The twins suddenly heard loud voices coming from the next room. It was easy to hear everything since only slotted wooden doors separated the two rooms.

"I thought I told you never to come here!" Jennifer said.

"Hey, hey," a male voice jeered. "I figured you'd be as pleased as punch to see me."

"Let's get one thing straight, Ricky," she said. "It may be true that I've agreed to enter into a 'business relationship' with you. But don't believe, even for a second, that that means I'll *ever* be 'happy' to see you."

Ricky laughed a cold, mean laugh. "Aw, you're just a little stuck up, that's all. You'll come around." He strutted over to her and slung his arm around her waist.

She stepped away and looked at him through eyes burning with anger. "Do you think I could ever be interested in a *blackmailer*?"

THE POPCORN PROJECT

Cynthia Blair

FAWCETT JUNIPER • NEW YORK

RLI: $\dfrac{\text{VL: 5 \& up}}{\text{IL: 6 \& up}}$

A Fawcett Juniper Book
Published by Ballantine Books
Copyright © 1989 by Cynthia Blair

Library of Congress Catalog Card Number: 88-92197

ISBN 0-449-70309-6

Manufactured in the United States of America

First Edition: April 1989

One

"Oh, no! Sooz, do you see what I see?"

Christine Pratt stopped in her tracks, right in front of the huge display window of Stark's Stationery Store. Her twin sister, Susan, hurried over to her side, anxious to see what all the fuss was about. But as she studied the attractive arrangement of spiral notebooks, ball-point pens, and brightly colored folders, she couldn't figure out why on earth Chris was getting so upset.

"What is it, Chris?"

"Just *look* at that!" Chris groaned loudly as she pressed her nose against the glass.

Puzzled, Susan studied the display even more carefully, trying desperately to find something unusual in the assortment of school and office supplies in the stationery store's window. But she remained confused.

"I'm afraid I still don't get it," said Susan. "All I see is a bunch of pens and pencils, and some looseleaf paper and binders, and a whole bunch of file folders and index cards. . . ."

"But that's just the point!" Chris wailed. "Pens, notebooks, pencils. . . . And as if that weren't bad enough, look at the apples and all those autumn leaves that Mr. Stark used to decorate the display!"

Susan just shook her head. "Sorry, Chris. You've lost me. I'm afraid I really can't see what all the fuss is about."

"Sooz, it's a back-to-school display!" exclaimed Chris. "And I, for one, am anything but ready for summer to be over!"

While Susan suddenly understood Chris's dismay, and was even a little bit sympathetic, she couldn't help chuckling over her twin sister's flair for the dramatic. It was a warm, sunny afternoon in the middle of August, and the seventeen-year-old Pratt twins were strolling down First Street after having just spent a few pleasant hours swimming at the Whittington Town Pool. They were taking their time, talking and laughing and just enjoying their relaxed mood as they made their way home, still wearing their bathing suits under shorts and baggy T-shirts, their towels and sun-tan lotion tucked into the red-canvas tote bag that Susan was carrying.

But suddenly that relaxed mood had vanished. Instead, Chris was moaning about the display of school supplies she had just happened upon, and Susan, trying to suppress her urge to giggle, wanted to comfort her.

"But Chris," Susan said calmly, "you know that Mr. Stark always starts putting back-to-school supplies in his store much too early. Why, it's only the second week in August! We've still got a full three weeks of summer left!"

Susan's reminder that there were, indeed, still three full weeks of summer left did help Chris feel a little bit better. Even so, she remained thoughtful as the two teenage girls continued walking home.

"Well, no matter what the calendar looks like," Chris finally said with a sigh, "I can't help feeling that the summer's *fun* is over. It's true that we've still got a few more weeks left, but we'll probably end up spending most of it getting ready to go back to school in the fall. You know, getting new clothes, having our hair cut . . . and buying some of those pens and notebooks and folders over at Stark's Stationery Store!"

"Maybe *you'll* be needing those things, Chris, since you're starting *college* in New York," Susan couldn't help saying in a teasing tone, "but the only back-to-school supplies that *I'll* be needing are paints and brushes and sketch pads!"

It was true that when the identical twins started another school year in just a few more weeks, they would not be needing the same kinds of things. After all, while both Pratt girls would be going off to New York City to continue their education, the routes they would each be following would be very different.

Chris was going to begin her freshman year at the University of New York. There she would be taking courses that would help her toward her goal: going on to law school to become an attorney.

Susan, meanwhile, would be starting art school at the Morgan School of Art, also in New York City. Attending art school had been a dream of hers ever since she was a little girl. While her outgoing sister wanted to use her friendly, talkative personality and her interest in people and their problems to pursue a career as a lawyer, Susan loved drawing and painting. Her goal was to become a professional artist.

The great variation in the careers that the identical twins had chosen to pursue was only one of the many differences between Christine and Susan Pratt. The two girls did look the same, with their thick chestnut brown hair, sparkling dark brown eyes, and pretty features, including ski-jump noses that gave them both an impish look. But the personalities behind the two look-alikes' appearance could scarcely have been more unalike.

Chris was always caught up in a whirl of social activity. She had dozens of friends, and she made a point of being involved in as many activities as she could possibly handle. During the school year, she had been on the Whittington High School swim team, as well as the cheerleading squad, yet had always found time to be on some committee or other, planning a school dance, a class picnic, or a fund-raising bake sale or car wash.

Susan, meanwhile, was quiet and shy, and preferred reading a good book or sketching or playing with the girls' pet cat, Jonathan, to talking on the phone or running for class president. While she, too, had many friends, she was much more thoughtful—and much more cautious.

Despite the girls' many differences, however, they did have one major thing in common. They both loved an adventure. They had a long history of playing pranks, more often than not calling upon their identical appearances to pull off capers that one person alone would have been unable to carry off. While doing so was always a lot of fun, it was never more rewarding than when one of their little schemes resulted in doing some good for someone who needed help.

For example, earlier that same summer, they had come to the aid of the residents of a resort island that was on the verge of ruin, as well as turning around the lives of two little girls who lived on that island, all by devising a plot they nicknamed the *Double Dip Disguise*. The summer before, they helped save a children's summer camp from having to close by solving the mystery behind some peculiar goings-on at Camp Pinewood. They nicknamed that summer *Strawberry Summer*. There were other adventures as well, each one of them an exciting new challenge—and each one achieving a reward that made the girls conclude that despite the risks they had taken, it had been worthwhile.

Today, however, as they made their way home, neither Chris nor Susan was thinking about their past adventures. Instead, they were both pondering the fact that the remaining days of their summer vacation were numbered—and it didn't look as if there was anything even close to adventurous ahead of them. And as if that weren't bad enough, the next store window that caught their eye contained a display of travel posters.

"Just look at those posters!" Chris cried, stopping once again, this time in front of the Near and Far Travel Agency. In the window were huge color photographs of exotic islands with palm trees and fine golden sand, dramatic castles perched upon flower-covered mountains, and busy city scenes in which the street signs were all in foreign languages.

"Why, just think of all the exciting places there are in the world! Hawaii, France, California . . . I don't suppose there's any chance we could sneak in a little trip before we go off to school, is there?"

"I'm afraid not, Chris." Susan laughed sympathetically, but she, too, was beginning to experience the same disappointment that her twin sister was. "I guess you and I will just have to wait until we go off to New York before we have any more adventures!"

"Well, maybe there aren't any adventures in store for me in the near future," said Chris, her eyes already beginning to twinkle mischievously, "but there is one thing I'm really beginning to look forward to."

"Really? What's that?"

"A shower! I don't know about you, Sooz, but these damp bathing suits and the chlorine from the pool are starting to make something as simple as a quick shower sound pretty enticing."

Susan chuckled. "You're absolutely right. And

do you know what other 'simple' thing is starting to sound better and better every second?"

"No, what?"

"A big glass of icy lemonade!"

"Oh, boy! I can hardly wait! Tell you what, Sooz; I'll race you home."

"You're on!"

It was just a few minutes before the two girls reached the Pratts' house, squealing and giggling and almost completely out of breath as they bounced through the front door, teasing each other about who was the actual winner of their little race. Even so, they had already forgotten all about the blue mood that had descended over them as they mournfully contemplated the fact that it looked as if the remainder of their summer had little in store for them besides getting ready for autumn.

Still laughing and joking, they burst into the kitchen in search of two tall glasses of homemade lemonade—then clasped their hands over their mouths. They looked at each other guiltily as they realized that their mother was sitting on a stool, talking on the telephone.

"Ooops!" cried Chris.

"Sorry, Mom," Susan whispered. She tiptoed over to the kitchen table and dropped into a chair.

Meanwhile Chris headed for the refrigerator. She was planning to grab the pitcher of lemonade, pick up two glasses, and then head out to the backyard in order to give the girls' mother some privacy—and some silence in which to talk.

Her mother's side of the conversation, however, caught her interest right away.

"But that's terrible, Karen!"

"Is thát Aunt Karen, your sister in California?" Chris whispered loudly. "What happened?"

Her mother just waved a silencing hand in her direction. "But you saw a doctor, right?"

"Mom, is Aunt Karen all right?" Susan demanded.

Once again, Mrs. Pratt was too involved in her telephone conversation to be interrupted.

"Oh, no! It's *broken*? Karen, how on earth are you going to manage for the next few weeks?"

"Mom!" the twins wailed. They went over to the phone, refusing to be left out for a moment longer. "What *happened*?"

Mrs. Pratt looked up and saw the concerned looks on her daughters' faces. "Hold on a minute, Karen." To the girls, she said, "Yes, it's Aunt Karen. She's broken her ankle, and since she lives alone, she's going to have a difficult time taking care of herself. . . . Wait, why don't you talk to her?"

"I'll pick up on the extension," Chris offered. Without waiting another second, she deposited the pitcher of lemonade on the counter and dashed out of the room, bounding toward the stairs.

By the time she reached the phone in the hallway on the second floor of the Pratts' house, Susan and her aunt were already engaged in an animated conversation.

"Well, you certainly don't sound too upset by all this," Susan was saying.

"The worst is over now," replied their favorite

aunt cheerfully. "The hard part is going to be managing on my own for the next few weeks. I have to use crutches to get around. Work will be no problem, since the daily cartoon strip I write for the *Los Angeles Star* doesn't involve anything besides sitting at my drawing table and trying to be clever— easy enough to do while stuck in a chair!

"But as for the day-to-day errands—buying food, cooking meals, doing laundry—well, I have yet to figure out how I'm going to manage. Oh, sure, my friends have been helpful so far. Even so, they have their own jobs and their own lives. . . ."

"That's too bad," Susan said sympathetically.

"It sounds like a tough situation," Chris agreed.

"Well, you two are the clever pranksters," Aunt Karen went on to tease. "Maybe you can come up with some solution to my problem!"

"Gee, I don't know." Susan was thoughtful. "We live so far away. . . . What can we do?"

"Yes, that's a tough one, even for two old pros like us," said Chris.

"Oh, well." Aunt Karen sighed. "It was worth a try. Don't worry about me, though; I'll find some way to manage. Perhaps I'll hire someone, some-body like a private nurse. Sure, it'd be expensive, but I really don't have much choice at this point."

The threesome chatted for a few more minutes, then said their good-byes. As far as Susan and Chris were concerned, however, the discussion of their aunt's problem was anything but over.

"Poor Aunt Karen!" Chris cried, flopping onto her bed.

Her twin followed her into the bedroom, sitting down on the edge of the windowseat after moving aside the dozen or so record albums that Chris had left there.

"Yes, it's such a shame. And as if the pain of having a broken ankle weren't bad enough in itself, now she has to deal with finding someone to take care of her."

"Oh, if only she lived closer!" Chris frowned. "It would be so easy for you and me to help Aunt Karen, doing her shopping and laundry and all that. It wouldn't even take that many hours a day! But we're so far away. . . ."

"Well," Susan mused, staring out the window, "maybe you and I should hop on the very first plane to Los Angeles and move in with her for a couple of weeks, until she can get around a little bit more easily."

She was barely thinking about what she said, instead concentrating on the Pratts' next-door neighbors who, at the moment, were busily planting an entire row of brand-new bushes that had just been delivered by the local nursery.

And so she was astonished by the reaction that her offhanded comment elicited.

"Sooz, that's it!"

"Huh?" Susan blinked as she looked back at her sister, having already forgotten what their discussion was about as she watched with amusement as the small green hedge that Mr. Hobson had just planted leaned over and fell onto the ground.

"You're absolutely right! That's *exactly* what we should do!"

"Hmmm? What should we do? I'm sorry. Chris; I wasn't really listening. You see, Mr. Hobson just planted this funny little bush and . . ."

"Let's do it, Sooz! Let's hop on a plane and go out to California! It's the perfect solution. And not only would we be able to help out Aunt Karen," she added, her brown eyes twinkling mischievously, "we'd be able to squeeze in just a little bit more summer fun before heading back to school in three more weeks! We could soak up some of that famous California sun, and see some of the tourist sights in the city . . . that is, if we could find the time, what with having to take care of Aunt Karen and all. . . . Hey, maybe we'd even get to meet some movie stars! *That* would be the most exciting thing of all!"

Susan's mouth dropped open. "Are you serious, Chris? Do you really think we should just rush out there?"

"Why not?"

"Well, think of how much it would cost, for one thing."

"Hmmm. You've got a point." But Chris came up with an answer to her sister's objection almost immediately. "I know. Maybe Aunt Karen will help pay our way, since we *would* be going out there mainly to help her!" She shrugged as she said, "After all, if she hired somebody, the way she said she probably would, that would be expensive, too. Maybe she'd just as soon 'hire' us by paying part of our air fare!"

Susan was wearing a huge grin as she said,

"Well, Chris, it's certainly worth a try! Shall we go call Aunt Karen back?"

Just as they'd been hoping, Karen was thrilled with the idea of having her two favorite nieces fly out to California to help her manage. And she thought the idea of helping pay their way was an excellent plan.

"Then it's settled," Aunt Karen said firmly. "Aside from the fact that I need as much help as I can get, I can't wait to see you girls! It's been years!"

"I can hardly believe it!" Chris cried, talking on the upstairs extension once again. "And here Sooz and I were just complaining about how the summer was just about over— "

"And how we wouldn't have any more adventures . . ." Susan piped up from downstairs in the kitchen.

"Not even any *fun*!" Chris exclaimed. "All we've been planning to do for the rest of August is buy new shoes and get our hair trimmed. . . ."

"We'd much rather come to California!" said Susan. "We can get our hair trimmed out there!" Suddenly she grew serious. "But there's one thing we forgot, Aunt Karen."

"What's that?"

"We forgot to ask Mom. We'll have to clear it with her, first."

Suddenly Aunt Karen burst out laughing.

"What's so funny?" both Chris and Susan demanded.

"I don't think you'll have any problem with your

mother saying yes to this idea," Karen said once she was able to gain control again. "After all, she and I just spent ten minutes on the phone agonizing over how we could possibly get you two to offer to fly out here and help me for a couple of weeks!"

"You mean you *tricked* us?" Chris cried, by now laughing herself.

"It looks like we've been outsmarted, Chris," Susan said with a chuckle. "It seems that you and I aren't the only pranksters in this family! Mom and Aunt Karen are pretty good at plotting their own little schemes!"

"Whether we were 'tricked' or not," said Chris, "I can't wait. California, here I come!"

"We'll start packing as soon as we hang up," said Susan. "Goodness, what should we bring?"

"Well, let's see." Aunt Karen thought for a few seconds. "Make sure you each bring a bathing suit. Lots of my friends have swimming pools, and of course there's the big old Pacific Ocean, just a fifteen-minute drive from my house."

"I'll bring two," said Susan.

"And I'll bring *three*!" Chris cried.

"All right. Bring a few sundresses. The weather is gorgeous—very warm, but not at all humid—so they'll be the most comfortable. Oh, and don't forget to bring comfortable shoes. Preferably sandals. You'll both be doing a lot of walking, I'm sure."

"What do you mean?" asked Susan.

"Well, you two don't expect to wait on me hand and foot all day, do you? And as much as I'm looking forward to seeing you both, I think that two energetic teenage girls can find other things to do in an exciting city like Los Angeles besides sitting around, talking to an old-timer like me. Besides going to the beach, we have movie studios you can tour, and Olvera Street in the old Mexican part of town, and some wonderful new art museums. And of course Disneyland is only an hour away. . . ."

Chris could contain herself no longer. "I can hardly wait! Aunt Karen, when do we leave?"

"Your plane reservations are for tomorrow at noon."

Susan's mouth dropped open. "Wait a minute, Aunt Karen," she said slowly. "What do you mean, our plane reservations are for tomorrow at noon?"

"You mean they've already been made?" asked Chris.

"See?" teased Aunt Karen. "I told you that your mother and I were pretty skillful pranksters! We had every confidence that you two would fall for our little plan—and you did!"

Aunt Karen suddenly grew serious. "There *is* one tiny condition, however. . . ."

"What's that?" both girls wanted to know.

"Your mother wants you to promise that there'll be no pranks, no tricks, no schemes, none of your little 'adventures.' With you two girls so far away from home, she said that she and your father would just worry too much. . . ."

"It's a deal!" Susan was quick to agree.

"Nothing but fun." Chris was equally enthusiastic. "We promise! Oh boy, Sooz! We're going to California!"

Even as the girls hung up the telephone and rushed into their bedrooms to start packing, they had no idea that while at the moment they both intended to hold up their end of the bargain, the Pratt twins were about to embark upon still one more of their memorable—and more than a little bit dangerous—adventures.

Two

"I can't believe we're really here," breathed Chris. She leaned across her sister so that her nose was pressed against the window of the airport bus. "Look! There it is! The city of Los Angeles! And it looks exactly the way I always imagined it would."

"I know. Look at all those palm trees."

"And that gorgeous California sunshine . . ."

"And the beautiful flowers everywhere . . ."

"Let's not forget the thing that Los Angeles is probably *most* famous for."

Susan glanced over at her twin, puzzled. "What's that, Chris?"

"Why, the network of highways and freeways that stretches out all over the place."

As the twins were chuckling over Chris's observation, one which happened to be right on target, they suddenly heard a deep voice behind them say,

"It sounds as if you girls are visiting Los Angeles for the first time."

"That's right. We are." Chris peeked over the back of her seat and found that she and her sister were sitting in front of a good-looking boy with blond hair, blue eyes, broad shoulders, and a wonderful tan—someone, in short, who looked exactly the way she always imagined California boys were supposed to look. As a matter of fact, she couldn't resist the temptation to tease him. "Don't tell me. You come from LA, right?"

The boy laughed. "Is it that obvious? Well, you're right. It just so happens that I was born and raised right here in the City of Angels. My name's Bruce Jackson. And where are you two from?"

The twins told Bruce about the small town of Whittington that they called home, explaining that they were visiting for two weeks in order to help care for their aunt who had just broken her ankle. When he heard their reason for coming to California, the boy frowned.

"Gee, it doesn't sound as if you two are going to be able to have very much fun while you're here, what with having to take care of a sick relative and all."

Susan and Chris looked at each other—and burst out laughing.

"What's so funny?" Bruce looked bewildered.

"First of all," Chris said patiently, "this 'sick relative' of ours is more fun than just about anybody we know. As a matter of fact, she's a cartoonist. She does a daily comic strip for one of the L.A. newspapers, the *Los Angeles Star*."

"Second of all," Susan continued for her twin, "she's not going to need *that* much attention. We'll have plenty of time to go off on our own and see the sights. . . ."

"*And* look for movie stars," Chris reminded her. "Don't forget about that. I'm not leaving this city until I have at least three celebrity autographs! But there's one more thing. Don't forget to tell Bruce that third of all, we Pratt twins *always* manage to have fun, no matter what we're doing!"

"Well, then, in that case, maybe you two will find the time to let me show you around a little bit. Check out some of the tourist attractions like Disneyland and Knott's Berry Farm, meet some of the kids who live out here . . . and I know some terrific beaches. Maybe you girls would like to give surfing a try."

"I think we can find the time to do some of those things," Chris said with a twinkle in her brown eyes.

Susan nudged her twin in the side with her elbow. Even though the girls had only been talking to Bruce for ten minutes or so, it was obvious to her that her sister had already taken quite a shine to this blond, muscular "California boy."

"By the way," Bruce went on casually, "maybe I've got an overactive imagination or something, but are you two . . . ?"

"You guessed it," said Chris with a chuckle. "Susan and I are identical twins. And I'm kind of surprised that you noticed. When she and I are dressed the way that each one of us feels most comfortable dressing, we hardly look the same at all."

"Well, then," Bruce teased, "let's just say that the image that we California boys have as expert 'girl-watchers' is one hundred percent true!"

The twins chatted with Bruce a little while longer, then exchanged phone numbers as they reached the hotel that was their drop-off point. From there, they took a taxi to Aunt Karen's house. Their thrill over having their initial glimpse of this exciting city had not yet worn off. In fact, they both kept their noses glued to the windows, with Susan trying to take in as much as she could—and Chris desperately trying to spot a movie star.

"Hey, Sooz, look at that man standing over there, in that parking lot! Isn't he that famous actor from the spy movies . . . ?"

"Chris," Susan informed her with a groan, "not only is his hair a different color; he's about six inches shorter than the movie star you're thinking of!"

"Well . . . maybe," Chris admitted, still peering eagerly at the faces of everyone she saw, "but I'm not going to give up. Sooner or later, you and I are going to see some real movie stars! After all, this is Los Angeles . . . the city in which Hollywood is located."

The taxi ride gave them quite a different perspective on the sprawling city. As they got closer and closer to Aunt Karen's apartment, they saw that there was a side to Los Angeles that was considerably less "glamorous" than what they'd been imagining. They passed schools, libraries, stores, houses and apartment complexes; all signs that— aside from the glittery movie industry and the exciting beach life they had heard so much about— this large city was also simply *home* to a lot of people.

By the time the taxi pulled up in front of a small complex of attractive two-story apartment buildings surrounded by palm trees and lush flowering plants, the twins could hardly wait to see their aunt. They rushed out of the cab, suitcases in hand, then quickly found the apartment that belonged to Karen.

"Hello! We're here!" they called, letting themselves in.

Just as they'd expected, they found Aunt Karen sitting at her drawing table, working away. Her left ankle was in a cast, and she had propped it up so that it was resting on a small footstool. Leaning on the wall next to her was a pair of crutches.

"Well, aren't you two a sight for sore eyes?" Karen put down her drawing pen and smiled warmly. "Getting you both out here, once and for all, was probably *worth* going out and getting this silly ankle of mine broken!"

"Oh, I don't know about that," Chris teased. "You could have just *invited* us, you know."

"Oh, Aunt Karen, it's so great to see you!" said Susan, setting down her suitcase and rushing over to give her aunt a hug.

"And we're pretty glad to be here in California, too," Chris added, following close behind.

After they had greeted each other with enthusiastic hugs and kisses and Karen had asked the twins a dozen questions about themselves and their parents, the older woman asked, "So, girls, what do you think of Los Angeles so far?"

Susan and Chris looked at each other and smiled.

"It certainly is big!" Susan replied.

After serving up cold drinks all around, the girls showed themselves around their new home. It was large and sunny, with a pleasant feeling of airiness that came from the many windows, the pastel color scheme, and the huge plants that Karen had tucked into nearly every corner of the one-bedroom apartment.

"I'd like you two to stay in the bedroom," Karen called in to them as they strolled into that room and found it just as pretty as the rest of the place. "I've been finding it easier just to sleep out here on the couch." By way of explanation, she added, "It's not easy, getting around on crutches. This way, I'm a lot closer to my drawing table—and the kitchen."

"From now on, you won't have to move at all," Susan assured her as the twins returned. "We'll do everything for you."

"That's right," Chris agreed. "Now, where would you like us to start?"

Karen looked at her two nieces in surprise. "My goodness, you two don't waste any time, do you?"

"Nope," said Chris with a grin. "Not when somebody needs us to help out. I'm afraid that whenever that happens, Sooz and I just can't resist sticking our noses into other people's business."

"Well, in that case, I'd suggest that you two help by making sure there's ice in the freezer and plenty of cups and napkins."

"That's a strange request!" Susan observed. "What on earth for?"

"Because," Aunt Karen explained with a smile, "in about half an hour, two dozen of my friends are coming over with food for a potluck supper. When they heard you were coming all the way from Whittington, they decided that a welcoming party would be just the thing—and they felt that filling up the house with their own delicious homemade food would make the next few days that much easier on two out-of-towners and an invalid."

"Oh, boy!" cried Chris. "A party! What better way to be introduced to an exciting new city like Los Angeles!"

Within an hour, Aunt Karen's apartment was filled with people—as well as so much food that the twins concluded they wouldn't have to cook a single meal for at least a week. It was fun playing hostess, even in a home that was theirs only temporarily.

They began by greeting each guest at the door, but as people continued to stream in, the twins finally decided just to leave the front door open. They were too busy dealing with all the casseroles and cakes and other delicacies that Karen's thoughtful friends kept delivering. In between unwrapping the food and arranging it all on her dining-room table, buffet-style, they tried to talk to everyone, finding this varied collection of Californians a fascinating group.

"Do you see that woman over there?" Susan whispered to her twin as the two of them busily took the aluminum foil off the latest dish that had arrived, one that had been presented to them by a glamorous-looking couple who quickly disappeared into the growing crowd of guests at this impromptu little party. "Aunt Karen just told me that she's one of the top reporters for the *Los Angeles Star*!"

"How thrilling!" said Chris. "And she told me that that man over there runs a fancy spa just north of the city. This is certainly one of the most exciting parties I've ever been to!"

"Maybe a movie star or two will even show up," Susan said.

But before her sister had a chance to respond, another guest arrived, this one bearing a bowlful of guacamole, a delightful dip made from avocados, tomatoes, and onions. While Chris took charge of this newest addition to their growing buffet, Susan wandered back into the living room, hoping to meet some more of Aunt Karen's friends.

She was standing in the doorway, looking over the crowd, when she heard someone say, "Excuse me. Could you please give me a hand with this?"

Susan turned around and found herself face to face with a pretty young woman with long blond hair and large green eyes. She looked as if she were about the same age as the twins, yet she had a special spark about her that was difficult not to notice. At the moment, however, she looked confused about what to do with the large rectangular dish, covered tightly in foil, that she was carrying.

"I don't know where to put this," the girl went on, "and you look as if you're one of the hostesses."

"It does look that way, doesn't it?" said Susan. "But actually, I'm as much a guest here as you are. My sister and I are just out here to help Aunt Karen for a while, since she broke her ankle."

"Oh, yes. I heard all about your aunt's terrible accident. You see, she and I have only met a few times; it's my father who's Karen's close friend. I just came along tonight because my father invited me."

"Well then, welcome! The more the merrier, I always say."

The young woman smiled, and Susan could see that she was really quite beautiful, even more striking than she had noticed at first. "Thank you. By the way, my name is Jennifer Franklin."

"Hello, Jennifer. I'm Susan Pratt."

"Hello, Susan." She laughed. "I'd shake your hand, but I'm afraid I've got my hands rather full right now."

"Oh, of course. Here, come into the kitchen. We can unwrap whatever it is you were kind enough to bring."

"It's a vegetable casserole—one of my specialties. Actually, it's one of the few decent things that I can make. Here, this could use some reheating before it's served."

"Fine. I'll just turn on the oven. Have you lived in Los Angeles all your life?"

As Susan chatted with her new acquaintance in

the kitchen, Chris brought a large bowl of tortilla chips out into the living room, the perfect accompaniment for the guacamole. Then she circulated through the room, making sure that their guests had enough ice in their drinks and enough silverware and napkins to enjoy the bountiful spread of food. She stopped to chat with as many people as she could, always keeping an eye out for her aunt, to make sure that she was comfortable and had everything she needed.

She was about to go back to the kitchen to get more paper napkins when she heard a friendly voice say, "Excuse me, but am I seeing double or is there another young woman at this party who looks exactly like you?"

Chris laughed. "No, you're not seeing double," she told the tall, dignified-looking man who was standing beside her, looking a bit puzzled. "My sister, Susan, and I are identical twins."

"Oh, I see. Are you friends of Karen's?"

"More than that. We're her nieces. Karen and our mother are sisters. When Aunt Karen broke her ankle, Sooz and I flew out here to give her a hand."

"Ah. So *you're* one of the famous nieces from Whittington! I didn't realize you were identical twins. Well, it was certainly nice of you both to volunteer to come all the way out here to help Karen."

"Well . . ." Chris couldn't help chuckling. "Doing a good deed for our aunt was only part of it. The chance to come to Los Angeles for a vacation had at least *something* to do with our willingness to come. After all, this is one place I've always wanted to see."

"I hope you're not disappointed. And if I can be of any assistance, just let me know." The man extended his hand. "I'm Donald Franklin."

"Hello, Mr. Franklin. I'm Christine Pratt. Everybody calls me Chris."

"And here comes your sister. My goodness! You two *do* look the same."

"Here, I'll introduce you. Susan, come on over and meet another one of Aunt Karen's friends. This is Donald Franklin."

"Hello," Susan said pleasantly. "I believe I just met your daughter, Jennifer."

"Ah, yes. Did you get her autograph?" he said with a teasing grin.

"Her autograph! Why, is she famous?"

"Not yet, but she may well be someday. Didn't she tell you she wants to be a movie actress?"

"No, she didn't. My goodness! How exciting!"

"Wow, a movie star—my very first one!" Chris cried. "Maybe I *will* ask her for her autograph. What movies has she been in?"

"Well, none . . . at least not yet. But she's taking acting classes, studying really hard. And during the day she works at Silver Screen Studios."

"What's this about Silver Screen Studios?" Aunt Karen, who happened to be sitting nearby, craned her neck toward the threesome in order to join their conversation. "Is Donald telling you some exciting inside information about the movie industry, the kind of thing only a major executive like him would know?"

Susan and Chris's mouths both dropped open.

Aunt Karen went on, "Next week, Donald here will be celebrating his twenty-fifth anniversary as a Silver Screen Studios employee. They're holding a big party in his honor.

"Gee," said Chris, "maybe I should get your autograph, too!"

"No, not me," Mr. Franklin insisted with a smile. "I'm happy to work behind the scenes, without any of the glory. But I am proud of the studio. Perhaps I can even talk you two into coming over to take the tour."

"Oh, I'd love to!" Chris cried. The look on her twin's face told her that the feeling was unanimous.

"Just make sure these two are escorted the entire time," Karen teased. "If the famous Pratt twins are left on their own for more than five minutes, Silver Screen Studios may never be the same again."

Mr. Franklin looked surprised. "What's this? Do you mean to tell me that these two girls are capable of mischief?"

"Well, not mischief, exactly," said Karen. "As a matter of fact, I must admit that all their shenanigans always seem to have a happy ending. Sometimes even more than that."

"Donald Franklin shook his head. "I'm sorry, but I'm afraid I still don't follow."

"Here, why don't you tell them, Chris and Susan? In the meantime, I'm going to hobble over to the buffet table and thank some of my friends for coming—and for bringing all this wonderful food. Why, we won't have to do any cooking for the next month."

"So what's all this about your adventurous past?" Mr. Franklin asked.

"Well," said Susan, blushing, "Karen was right when she said that Chris and I have a way of getting involved in pranks and disguises and things like that. But," she was quick to add, "it's almost always for a good cause! We do like to help people out, whenever we can. As a matter of fact, whenever we hear that somebody has a problem, we can hardly resist."

"That's right," Chris went on. "It all started when Sooz and I decided to try switching places, to see what each other's life was like. We even had a nickname for that first adventure of ours: the *Banana Split Affair*."

"That's because we made a bet with each other over whether or not we'd be able to pull it off," Susan told him, "and the stakes were a banana split."

"And did you manage to carry it off?" asked Mr. Franklin with a smile.

"We sure did." Just thinking about that little escapade made Chris chuckle. "Anyway, once we found out we could do it—switch places, I mean— there was no stopping us. We started to use our identical appearances to help us solve mysteries and do all kinds of things."

"Go on," said Mr. Franklin. "Tell me more."

Susan and Chris were only too happy to tell this kind man all about their past adventures. And then, when they had just about exhausted their supply of amusing stories, Mr. Franklin said something rather odd.

More to himself than to the twins, he muttered in a barely audible voice, "I wish I had a couple of sleuths like these girls to help *me* out."

It wasn't until later that the twins had a chance to discuss the two brand-new friends they had just made here in this brand-new city of Los Angeles— and the peculiar statement Mr. Franklin had made, one that they might not even have been meant to hear.

"Gee, Mr. Franklin seemed like an awfully nice man," Susan observed as the twins were alone in the kitchen, making the third pot of coffee of the evening. "His daughter, too. Jennifer is one of the sweetest people I've ever met. And just think. One day she might even be a famous actress!"

"Yes, they were nice," Chris said thoughtfully. "But did you catch that strange comment he made when we were telling him all about our sleuthing adventures? About how he wished he had a couple of people like us to help him out?"

"Yes, I did hear him say that." Susan frowned. "Gee, I wonder what he meant. It does sound as if he has some kind of problem, something he needs help with. . . ."

But before the girls had a chance to think about Mr. Franklin any more, another guest burst in, in search of a paper towel to mop up a spilled glass of ginger ale. Mr. Franklin, his interest in the girls' past adventures, and the odd comment he had made were all forgotten.

At least, for the moment.

Three

"*So, Sooz, what do you want to do today?*" *asked* Chris with a playful grin. "After all, this *is* our first day as tourists here in Los Angeles! What's it going to be? Shopping on Rodeo Drive, where some of the wealthiest people in the world shop? Touring Silver Screen Studios, as Mr. Franklin suggested? Or maybe going for a swim at one of those famous Southern California beaches?"

Susan glanced up from the glass of fresh orange juice she was drinking for breakfast. It was made from oranges she and her sister had picked off a tree in the yard behind their Aunt Karen's apartment less than fifteen minutes earlier, then squeezed into juice in the electric juicer that was on the counter. It was a delight for both girls, as well as for their aunt, who admitted as she was served breakfast in "bed" that she didn't always find the time to make herself fresh squeezed orange juice.

Now, the twins and their aunt were sitting together in the sunny living room, gazing out at the gorgeous view: the palm trees and lush flowers that surrounded the apartment complex, made even more breathtaking by the fact that they were bathed in the bright early-morning sunshine. As they drank fresh orange juice and admired the scenery, the threesome contemplated the day ahead.

"Well," Susan replied hesitantly, "don't you think we should wait to hear what Karen needs first, before we go ahead and make any plans? After all, our main reason for being here in the first place is to help her out."

"Do you mean I still haven't managed to convince you two that this helpless act of mine was just an excuse to get you both out here for a visit?" Karen teased. "At any rate, there are just a few things I'd like you to do for me before you go off on your own. Let's see; you could pick up a few things at the supermarket—here, I've made a list—and then stop off at the dry cleaners. . . . Oh, and I need some of these special drawing pencils. I wrote down the name and number. There's a small art-supplies store right down the street." She shrugged as she handed a small piece of paper to Chris. "Aside from those few errands, I should pretty much be set for the rest of the day."

As Chris glanced at the list, Susan looked around the small but prettily decorated apartment. "I'll tell you what, Aunt Karen. How about if Chris goes off and does your errands, and meanwhile I'll stay here and straighten up a little bit? There are still all the dishes from your party last night, and this kitchen floor looks as if it could use some sweeping. . . . Do you mind?"

"Mind? I should say not! As a matter of fact, I don't know what I'd do without you two angels of mercy!"

"Okay, then," said Chris. "You can just sit back and take it easy, Aunt Karen, and we'll do all the rest. Just leave everything to us."

Sure enough, in less than an hour, Chris had gone to both the dry cleaners and the art-supplies store, then stocked up on food at the supermarket. In addition to the items on her aunt's list, she had taken the liberty of adding a few extra items, things that to her embodied the healthful, and just a little bit exotic, feeling of southern California, foods like fresh avocados, mangos, and bean sprouts.

Susan, meanwhile, kept busy at Karen's. First she straightened up the whole apartment. Then she picked a huge bouquet of brightly colored flowers, pink and red and orange, and found a vase large enough to display them all in their glory.

"My goodness!" Karen commented, looking up from the drawing board that was set up in the sunniest corner of the living room. "You've already made such a difference. Having you two come out to visit was one of the best ideas your mother and I ever had."

So the twins were feeling quite pleased with the way things were going as they hopped into their aunt's car late that morning. They had finally agreed upon a destination, a place they were both anxious to see as well as one that seemed like a fitting way of officially beginning their tour.

"Disneyland is fantastic!" cried Chris, throwing out her arms to demonstrate just how thrilled she really was. All around her were the distinctive Victorian-style buildings of Main Street, the theme park's re-creation of an American town at the turn of the century.

There was an old-fashioned ice-cream parlor with a colorfully striped awning, an apothecary shop that looked as if it truly were from the turn of the century, and a candy store selling penny candy that looked too pretty to eat. An outdoor flower stall displayed bright bouquets of flowers, the perfect spot to snap a few pictures—which is exactly what the twins did. And in the midst of the "town" a red trolley trundled along on trolley tracks, and the twins could hardly wait for a ride.

After stopping to see a movie about Walt Disney, the girls had given in to the irresistible urge to do some shopping. At the moment, Susan was clutching a big, stuffed Minnie Mouse, originally intended as a gift for her aunt but something she was already becoming so attached to that she doubted she'd ever be able to part with it. Chris, meanwhile, was wearing a pair of Mouseketeer ears with her name embroidered across the front in gold thread.

"You're right; this place *is* amazing," Susan agreed enthusiastically. "I still can't believe we're really here. Where should we go next? Adventureland? Tomorrowland?"

"I don't know about you, Sooz," Chris said with a twinkle in her eye, "but just being here is making me feel like a kid again. I want to head over to Fantasyland!"

Over the next few hours, the Pratt twins soared through the air on the backs of identical Dumbos, explored the jungle in a wooden boat, went twenty thousand leagues under the sea to look at exotic deep-sea fish and a sunken ship dripping with treasure, roamed around a haunted house, and got a taste of the life of a Caribbean pirate. It was a wonderful day, filled with fun and fantasy, a teasing of the imagination that they would never forget.

When the girls arrived back at Karen's apartment, late that afternoon, clutching souvenirs not only for themselves and their aunt but also for their family and friends in Whittington, they were both tired from their day. In fact, they were actually looking forward to a quiet evening at home, resting up and telling their aunt all about the things they had seen and done that day.

So they were surprised when they walked in the front door and found that this day full of fun was anything *but* over.

"I want to hear all about your day, Susan and Chris," said Karen. She was stretched across the couch, her broken ankle elevated on a pillow as she read the newspaper. "But first, I have a telephone message for you."

"Who called?" asked Chris. "Mom and Dad?"

"Or maybe it was that cute boy you met on the airport bus," teased her twin. "Wasn't his name Bruce Jackson?"

"As a matter of fact, it was Mr. Franklin," Aunt Karen replied. "He was hoping you both would drop over to his house for a little visit. I'd come along myself, but I'm afraid I still have to finish up my cartoon strip for this weekend's funnies."

"Do you mean he wants us to come over *now*?" asked Chris, as pleased as she was surprised.

"Don't tell me you two tourists are already all tuckered out—and after only one day of sightseeing!" Aunt Karen teased. "Actually, when I mentioned that you'd gone to Disneyland today, he said he thought you might enjoy the chance to wind up your afternoon by relaxing in his pool. And then— if you're interested, of course—join Jennifer and him for dinner. How does that sound?"

Susan and Chris just looked at each other and grinned.

After calling Mr. Franklin back to firm up their plans, the twins showered and changed. While only a short time earlier, they had been complaining about how hot and tired they were, moaning dramatically over their tired feet, their new friend's invitation to spend the evening at his house made them as energetic as if they'd just had a full eight hours' sleep.

"I hope you don't mind us leaving you alone like this again, Aunt Karen," Susan said apologetically as she and her sister headed out the door once again, less than an hour after they'd gotten back to the apartment.

"Not at all," she assured them. "All I ask is two things."

"What's that?" asked Chris.

"First of all, that you tell me all about your evening—including your impressions of the Franklins' beautiful home. Just being there always makes me feel like I'm in a movie, rather than real life. It's one of those huge Beverly Hills mansions that I'm sure you've heard about."

"Fine," Susan agreed. "But what's the second thing?"

"The second thing," replied Aunt Karen with a big smile, "is that after dinner, you ask for a doggy bag for your leftovers. When Donald Franklin throws a dinner party, the results are never anything less than stupendous!"

Sure enough, it was just as Aunt Karen had promised; the Franklins' home was spectacular. It was a mansion in one of Los Angeles's most exclusive sections, Beverly Hills. It was a three-story white stucco house, surrounded by huge, colorful flowers and graceful palm trees. Behind the house was a huge swimming pool with a stone patio all around. Edging it was a high hedge with elegant marble statues peeking out from every one of the four corners.

Jennifer was on hand to greet them as they arrived, apologizing for the fact that her father was still at the studio.

"But don't worry; he'll be back soon," she was quick to assure them. "And it's not only because he's looking forward to seeing you two again," she went on with a teasing smile. "Tonight we're serving authentic Mexican food for dinner—one of my father's all-time favorites!"

The three young women enjoyed a relaxing swim, splashing about in the most beautiful surroundings the Pratt girls had ever seen. Just like their aunt, they, too, almost felt as if they were in a movie. It was certainly the perfect way to cool off after a long day of walking around in the hot August sun.

Jennifer proved to be a truly gracious hostess. She was also a pleasant conversationalist, enthralling Chris and Susan for almost an hour with her tales of what it was like to be an aspiring actress here in the movie capital of the world. The acting lessons, the auditions, the endless hours spent memorizing lines, the long workouts at the gym in order to keep in shape . . . it was all quite a bit more demanding than the twins had ever dreamed.

"Gee, it sounds difficult, trying to be a movie star," Chris whispered to her sister as they finally dragged themselves away from their new friend and strolled over to the poolside cabanas to change out of their wet bathing suits and into the crisp sundresses they'd brought along. "Learning all those lines, worrying about how your hair looks every minute of the day . . ."

"Yes, but if anyone can make it, Jennifer can," Susan insisted. "I bet she's really talented. Besides, you can tell that it means everything to her."

By the time dinner was served at an elegant white wrought-iron table next to the pool, the twins were ravenous. Mr. Franklin had joined the party by then, looking every bit the California host in his beige knit sportshirt and khaki pants.

"So, how was your first day as tourists here in our fantastic city?" he asked as the foursome dug into a sumptuous meal, consisting of huge plates of enchiladas, tacos, and burritos, all served with rice and beans. "I hope you haven't been disappointed so far."

"Oh, not at all!" Chris assured him. "Our first stop was Disneyland—and we loved it."

After they had given their two eager listeners an enthusiastic report on their day, Donald Franklin said, "Well, now, I'm more anxious than ever for you to take the tour of Silver Screen Studios. I'd say it's at least as much fun as a day at Disneyland. Besides," he added with a twinkle in his eyes, "maybe you'll even get to see some movie stars."

"But Daddy!" Jennifer protested. "They already have!"

"Who?" the other three asked in unison.

"Why, Donald Duck and Mickey Mouse!"

The rest of the evening proceeded just as pleasantly. The foursome continued to sit by the pool, watching the sensational sunset as they finished up their dinner with sopapillas, a special Mexican dessert made of delicately fried dough smothered in honey and topped with whipped cream.

It was quite late by the time the party began to show signs of coming to a close. After Jennifer and her father had gone inside, the twins lingered out on the patio, gathering up their damp bathing suits and towels so they could say good-night and be on their way. It was then that Chris said, "Boy, Sooz. This was easily the nicest dinner party I've ever been to."

"I know," Susan agreed with a sigh. "This whole evening has been perfect, hasn't it? And it's nice to see Jennifer and her father together. They seem to get along so well . . ."

Before she had even had a chance to finish her sentence, there came the sound of loud voices from inside the house. The twins looked up, startled.

"Daddy, who I see and what I do is none of your business!" From the tone of her voice, it sounded as if Jennifer was very angry.

"I know that, honey. And I'm not trying to pry. I'm just concerned, that's all." Mr. Franklin was attempting to be soothing, but it was apparent that he, too, was extremely upset.

"Well, I'm tired of all your questions! I know that you're watching me every minute, and . . . and listening in on my phone calls. . . ."

"Jennifer, I'm not! I hope you don't really believe I'd ever do anything like that. I'm just worried about you. You've been acting so . . . so *strange* lately."

"Maybe it's time I just packed my things and moved out," Jennifer countered. "Maybe I should get my own apartment, some place where I can have some *privacy*!"

There was the loud slamming of a door, followed by the sound of running.

A few seconds later, Mr. Franklin emerged. Despite his efforts to look calm, the girls could see how distraught he was.

"I'll—I'll have to see you girls to your car by myself," he said quietly. "I'm afraid that Jennifer has decided to retire early this evening."

Suddenly his expression changed. "Who am I trying to fool? I'm sure you both overheard our little argument just now."

Sheepishly, Chris and Susan nodded.

"I'm sorry. I've always believed that it was rude to burden guests with one's personal problems. But the truth is, Jennifer and I have been arguing so much lately that it was almost inevitable that you would end up witnessing one of our battles tonight."

"Is—is everything all right?" Susan asked gently.

Mr. Franklin shook his head sadly. "Actually, I'm not really sure. About two months ago, Jennifer started working at Silver Screen Studios—as you well know, the same studio where I work. I helped her get the job there as a tour guide. But beyond that, I have nothing to do with what she does there. What I mean is, I really have no way of knowing how she spends her time while she's at work, or who she sees. . . ."

"Why does that matter?" asked Chris, puzzled.

Mr. Franklin sighed deeply. "Because ever since she started working there, she's been acting very strange."

"Strange?" Susan repeated. "What exactly do you mean by strange, Mr. Franklin?"

"Jennifer and I have always been extremely close. She and I never had any problem discussing anything that was bothering her.

"But then she started going out with this new boyfriend of hers. At least, I assume he's her new boyfriend. Ricky Wheeler, I believe his name is. Ever since she started spending time with him, she's been quiet, withdrawn, maybe even a little bit secretive. I hate to say it, but it's almost as if she's been afraid to talk to me."

"Maybe she's in love," Chris suggested. "I know that every time I think I've met the boy of my dreams, I start acting pretty strange myself."

Mr. Franklin shook his head. "I'm afraid that's not it. No, I know Jennifer well enough to know that something is troubling her. Something important . . . and, as far as I can tell, something bad. Something is definitely wrong, and I'd give anything to know what it is."

Suddenly he looked up, startled. "My goodness! Why am I burdening you both with all this?" he said heartily. "It's been a long day, and I'm sure you're anxious to be on your way. Here, I'll walk you to your car."

As Chris and Susan drove back to their aunt's apartment, neither of them had very much to say. The city at night was beautiful. Enjoying the cool, fragrant air that wafted through the car's open windows, they gazed out at the towering palm trees that were all the more impressive by moonlight, especially against a backdrop of the bright lights of the various sections of this huge, sprawling city.

But as the twins sat in silence, it was not the beauty of the scenery that they were thinking about.

Once they were back at their aunt's place, Susan and Chris continued thinking about the two very different sides of the relationship between Jennifer and her father that they had witnessed this evening. It was obvious that they were close; at the same time, there was definitely something wrong.

"Gee, Sooz," Chris finally said, after they'd tiptoed into their aunt's pretty lavender-and-blue bedroom and began settling in for the night. "I feel so bad for Mr. Franklin. He's such a nice man. And it's obvious that he's really upset about his daughter."

"I feel bad for Jennifer, too," said Susan, climbing into bed and pulling the cool blue sheets up over herself. "She's someone who seems to have everything going for her, yet there's something so terrible bothering her that she doesn't even feel she can talk to her father about it."

Chris sighed loudly. "Two nice people like Jennifer and her father, having some kind of problem that they can't seem to work out by themselves. . . . Gee, I wish we could help them out."

Susan looked over at her and blinked. "What did you say, Chris?"

"Oh, I just said that I wish we could . . ." Suddenly, her dark brown eyes narrowed. "Susan Pratt, are you thinking what I *think* you're thinking?"

"I can't help it, Chris. It's just that when you said you wished we could help the Franklins, the first thought that popped into my head was, 'Well, why *can't* we?' "

"You've got a point, Sooz," Chris thought for a few seconds, her chin resting in her hands as she sat cross-legged on the bed. "It's not as if we don't have any experience doing this kind of thing."

"That's right. And it's clear that Mr. Franklin *wants* help. Why, remember just last night, at the party, when we were talking about our various escapades? He made that strange comment about how he wished he had a couple of sleuths like you and me to help him out. This must be what he was talking about."

"I think you're right. Well, then, what do you suggest that we do?"

Susan frowned. "Let's see. I guess we should start by finding out a little bit about Jennifer Franklin—where she goes, who she sees, what she does. . . ."

"Maybe we can even find out something about that new boyfriend of hers. What did Mr. Franklin say his name was?"

"Ricky Wheeler."

Chris nodded. "That's right. Well, I think we should give it a shot. I'd love to help out Mr. Franklin by finding out what's troubling his daughter. And, hopefully, help her out in the process.

"Besides," she went on, a twinkle in her eyes, "I've already got the perfect name for this project, this attempt of ours at trying to get to the bottom of all this."

Despite the serious tone of their discussion up until this point, Susan couldn't help chuckling. "All right, Chris. Let's hear it. What's your idea?"

"Well, Jennifer works at a movie studio, plus she wants to be in the movies herself one day, right?"

"Right."

"I don't know about you, Sooz, but whenever I think of going to the movies, I immediately think of one thing."

"Which is . . . ?"

"Popcorn! Therefore, I think we should nick-name this little caper 'the Popcorn Project.' "

"You're right; that *is* perfect. I love it, Chris. 'The Popcorn Project.' So we're agreed, then. First thing tomorrow morning, the Popcorn Project begins." Susan leaned over and turned off the light. "Now, Rule Number One in the sleuthing business is, Never start a new project unless you've had a full night's sleep. And I, for one, am ready for just that!"

The girls were quiet after that, lying in bed, waiting for sleep to descend upon them. Yet even though it was late, and they had both had a long and eventful day, neither of them could stop thinking about the fact that now that they'd agreed to tackle the Popcorn Project, there was a very good chance that they'd find out something that they'd rather not know about Jennifer Franklin. After all, she *did* appear to be in some kind of trouble. They were about to delve into something that someone their age—someone who, in fact, reminded them both of themselves a little bit—had chosen to keep a secret, even from her father, someone she loved very much.

And knowing that made it hard for either of them to fall asleep for a very, very long time.

Four

"Well, how do we look?"

Chris came bounding into the living room, bursting with enthusiasm. While it was still quite early in the morning, she found her aunt already working at her drawing board.

Karen glanced up from the comic strip she was working on and saw her niece standing before her, ready for inspection. Susan was not far behind.

"What do you think, Aunt Karen?" Chris repeated. "What I mean is, when you look at the two of us, what do you think we are?"

Karen surveyed the twins one at a time. Chris was wearing white cotton jeans and the pink T-shirt she had bought herself at the airport. Across the front, in purple, was scrawled *Los Angeles*. Susan, meanwhile, was dressed in a brightly colored flowered sundress and sandals, with a camera around her neck and a guidebook in her hand.

The twins' aunt couldn't keep from bursting out laughing.

"Why, you two look like typical California *tourists*."

"Oh, good!" Susan clapped her hands in glee.

"What a relief!" Chris agreed. "That's exactly what we're *trying* to look like."

"And here I would have thought you two would be trying to blend in," Karen teased. "You know, trying to pass yourselves off as native Californians, rather than out-of-towners."

"Oh, no!" Susan went on to explain. "You see, if we're going to spend the day following Jennifer Franklin, we *want* to look like tourists. That way, no one will think it's strange that we're hanging around Silver Screen Studios."

"*Wait* a minute." Karen put down her drawing pen and folded her arms across her chest. "I think I missed something. What do you mean, 'If we're going to spend the day following Jennifer Franklin'? What on earth are you talking about, Susan?"

The twins looked at each other guiltily.

"I guess we forgot to tell you about the Popcorn Project," said Susan.

"The *what*?"

The twins sat down on the couch. And then, matter-of-factly, Susan told their aunt all about the argument between Jennifer and her father that they'd overheard the night before, as well as what Mr. Franklin had said to them afterward. Chris then mentioned the strange comment he had made the night of the party, about how he wished he had a couple of sleuths to help him out. Finally, Susan finished up, telling Aunt Karen about their decision to come to their new friends' aid by finding out what was troubling Jennifer to see if they could help—a caper they had already nicknamed the Popcorn Project.

"After all," she said with a grin, "we Pratt twins never were very good at walking away from a challenge. Especially one that would give us the chance to help someone out."

"That's right," Chris interjected. "And this time, for all we know, we may even be helping out *two* people—Mr. Franklin *and* Jennifer."

"Well!" exclaimed Aunt Karen once the girls had finished. They looked at her expectantly, anxious to see what her reaction would be.

What she said, however, was not at all what they had expected.

"I guess your mother was right," said Karen.

The twins were puzzled.

"What do you mean, Aunt Karen?" asked Susan, frowning.

"Yes," echoed Chris. "What did our mother say?"

"That wherever you two go, some kind of adventure is almost sure to follow. But do me a favor, okay?"

"Sure," said Chris. "Anything."

Karen smiled ruefully. "Let's not mention the Popcorn Project to your parents . . . at least not yet. After all, they made me promise that I wouldn't let you two get involved in any of your mischievous little pranks while you were out here in California. And to tell you the truth, I wouldn't, if Donald Franklin weren't such a nice man—and such a good friend of mine."

The twins just looked at each other and grinned.

A half hour later, Chris was driving their aunt's car along one of the crowded, fast-moving Los Angeles freeways. Her sister sat beside her, studying a complicated map.

"Aside from the fact that we're going to be keeping an eye on Jennifer today," she said, after telling her sister they were about to reach the exit, "I'm really looking forward to taking the tour of Silver Screen Studios. I'm sure it'll be fascinating, seeing how they make movies. Just think. Wonderful costumes and makeup, special effects, huge lights and cameras . . . Gee, do you suppose we'll see any movie stars?"

"I sure hope so." As Chris glanced over at her sister, there was a twinkle in her dark brown eyes. "And just in case we do, I made certain I brought along a few pens and a pad of paper, just in case we have a chance to get somebody's autograph!"

When the girls arrived at Silver Screen Studios, they discovered that they were not the only ones who had scheduled a tour of this popular tourist attraction on this warm sunny day. They waited in a long line before getting inside. Then they were assigned to a tour group. After being seated in a "tram," a trainlike line of little cars that reminded them of one of the rides at Disneyland, their tour guide introduced himself.

"Good morning, and welcome to Silver Screen Studios!" said the good-looking young man who was standing at the front of the tram. His tall, thin frame was exaggerated by the kelly-green tour guide's uniform he was wearing, and as he spoke, his straight brown hair kept falling into his blue eyes. He was using a microphone to speak to the two dozen or so tourists who had been assigned to his group.

"My name is Henry Hartley, your guide during this morning's tour. You'll be seeing some exciting things today as I take you through the studios. You'll visit an entire Wild West town used in the filming of westerns. You'll stop off at the wardrobe department where you'll see hundreds of costumes, some of which you may recognize from movies you've seen. And at the end, there'll be a demonstration of some of the special effects used in making movies.

"Now, please feel free to ask any questions you may think of as we go along, and I'll try my best to answer them. Are you ready? Then let's go."

For the next hour and a half, Chris and Susan and the other members of Henry Hartley's tour group were treated to a tour of Silver Screen Studios that was, indeed, exciting—just as their charming and talkative tour guide had promised. In addition to the town from the Wild West and the wardrobe department, they also saw a warehouse full of sets and props, a stable full of every kind of car imaginable, including some that were real antiques, and an actual dressing room, one that had been used by an actor that the twins had heard of.

By the end of the tour, the twins couldn't imagine that there was anything left to see. Yet Henry informed them all that there was, indeed, still more—something that was, as far as he was concerned, the very best part.

"Gee, this has been fun," said Chris with a sigh. She and her twin were filing into a small theater with at least three hundred other tourists, all of whom were eager for this final segment of the tour, the demonstration of some of the special effects used in making motion pictures. "I'm sorry it's almost over—although I'm sure that, as Henry promised, the best is yet to come." Curious, she eyed the display of strange-looking equipment that was sitting up on the stage.

"Yes, it has been fun. But don't forget; we didn't come here only to have a good time," Susan reminded her sister. "We're supposed to be keeping an eye out for Jennifer Franklin, remember?"

Chris nodded. "Yes, of course. I haven't forgotten that for a single minute. But I'm beginning to realize that it may not be quite as easy as I first thought. Have you noticed that there are security guards posted all over the place?"

"And they look like they mean business, too." Susan sighed. "Maybe we're not going to be able to help out Mr. Franklin, after all. . . . Hey, wait a minute! Isn't that Jennifer over there?"

Chris craned her neck in the direction her sister had indicated. Already her heart was pounding. Sure enough—there she was, over at the other end of the theater, dressed in the same perky green uniform that their guide, Henry, was wearing. She, like him, was overseeing a group of about two dozen tourists, ushering them into the theater for the special-effects demonstration that marked the end of the Silver Screen Studios tour.

"That's her, all right." Chris clutched her twin's arm. "But it's not going to be easy, following her around, trying to keep an eye on her. Not with all these security guards around!"

"Even so," Susan said firmly, "we've *got* to find a way! After all, isn't that the main reason we came here today?"

Before her twin sister had a chance to reply, however, the lights in the theater suddenly grew dim. A hush fell over the crowd. For the moment, the Popcorn Project was simply going to have to wait.

"Good morning, ladies and gentlemen!" boomed a voice from the stage—a voice that belonged to none other than Henry Hartley, the girls were amused to discover. "All of the tour guides here at Silver Screen Studios hope you've enjoyed your tour this morning."

"But before you go, we'd like to present what we consider the highlight of the tour. We're going to demonstrate some of the special effects that are used in making movies. But first . . . oh, my. Not again!"

Henry looked just a little bit annoyed as the left arm of his green uniform suddenly burst into flames. While the audience's first reaction was one of alarm, they realized almost immediately, thanks to the calm expression on his face, that what they were seeing was not at all a dangerous situation, but merely the first special-effects demonstration.

"Yup, folks, you guessed it. This 'fire' isn't real; it's simply one of the special effects used in the movies. You've seen it all a million times . . . Even so, every time I have to demonstrate it, I get so mad!"

With that, he picked up a chair and banged it lightly on the floor. Immediately, it fell into a dozen pieces.

"Ah, yes," he went on. "One of those chairs that breaks with the slightest tap. Now, I know you've seen these, in just about every western you've ever watched. Some bad guy is always hurling these at a good guy, usually in a barroom brawl."

Already his audience was totally captivated. And Chris and Susan were no exception as they sat still, their eyes glued to the stage in fascination.

"The most important part of special effects is that they *look* dangerous—just like the real thing—but they don't actually *hurt* anybody. For example, say you were filming a movie and you wanted a couple of small explosions . . ."

Just then, in four different places throughout the auditorium, there were loud explosions, including a flash of light and a billow of smoke immediately afterward. After everyone in the audience jumped at the noise, they all laughed.

"See that? Now you're getting the hang of it. Not everybody has such a good sense of humor, though. Sir, why aren't you laughing? Sir? Sir?" Henry stepped off the stage and went over to a man sitting in the front row. "What's the matter, mister? Don't you have a sense of humor?"

With an angry look on his face, he picked up the gentleman in the front row with both hands and slammed him against the stage. Everyone gasped, then—when they realized that it was a wooden dummy that Henry assaulted—burst out laughing at their own willingness to believe what they knew, intellectually, to be fake.

Amidst the laughter, Henry shrugged. "See that, folks? The moral here is, Don't believe everything you see. In fact, maybe you should play it safe. Don't believe *anything* you see!"

Much to everyone's horror, Henry began to pull on his cheeks and forehead. Before hundreds of pairs of astonished eyes, Henry's face began to come off. It was just a mask! Then he reached up and pulled off a wig, revealing that, underneath the disguise, there was one of the young *female* tour guides!

As the *real* Henry Hartley stepped out from behind a curtain, where he had been supplying the voice that went with the mask, the audience broke into enthusiastic applause.

"Wow!" cried Susan. "That was really something!"

"I'll say!" Chris agreed. "They really had me fooled!"

"Now," said Henry and the other tour guide, who he had just introduced as Wendy, "are there any questions?"

Susan's hand shot up right away.

"You, in the back," said Henry.

"How exactly are those masks made?" she asked.

"It's a long process, actually. First, you make a plaster cast of the person's face. Then, you press the three-dimensional image into soft latex, a very thin sheet of rubber. Once the basic shape is in place, a highly trained artist paints in all the facial details."

"And how is it attached to the person who wears it?"

"Spirit gum. It's great stuff, and it allows the person wearing the mask to look very real. She can even move her mouth, just like Wendy here. Pretty convincing, don't you think?"

"And how about the fake fire?" Susan asked. "How exactly does that work?"

"I'm afraid we don't have any more time for questions," Wendy interjected politely. "It's time for the next group to come in. Thank you for coming, everyone. We hope you enjoyed touring Silver Screen Studios."

"That was great!" Susan said as she and her sister stood up and began to exit the auditorium with all the others. "Henry was right; it was the high point of the tour."

"It was pretty amazing," said Chris.

"Excuse me . . ." As the twins reached the back of the auditorium, Susan heard a voice right behind her. She turned around and found herself looking at Henry Hartley, who was wearing a wide, friendly grin.

"Yes?"

"You certainly asked a lot of questions in there!"

Susan could feel her cheeks turning pink. "Well, I guess I found the whole subject of special effects pretty fascinating."

"Yes, it is interesting, isn't it? As a matter of fact, I hope that when I finish college, I can get involved in the field."

"Really?" Susan was so intrigued by what Henry was saying that she forgot all about her sister who, only moments earlier, had been standing right next to her.

"That's right. In a few weeks, I'll be starting my freshman year at the University of Southern California, studying filmmaking techniques. And, well, maybe one day, I'll actually get to work in the movie industry."

"How exciting! Then I guess you really *didn't* mind me asking all those questions."

"Not one bit. But now it's my turn. I have a question for you."

"Really? What's that?"

"Well, since you're obviously a tourist here in our fair city of Los Angeles," Henry said with a grin, "I was wondering if maybe you'd enjoy having one of the locals show you around. How about a local who just happens to be a professional tour guide?"

Susan laughed. "I'd be honored."

"Great! How about starting with a concert tonight at the Hollywood Bowl?"

"What's that?" Susan asked, puzzled.

"It's a wonderful place, a huge outdoor amphi-
theater, where thousands of people can listen to
music under the stars. They have all kinds of con-
certs, too: classical music, rock, folk, pop . . .
something for everybody. I'm pretty sure there's
something worthwhile going on there tonight. As a
matter of fact, if we go a little bit early, we can even
bring along a picnic dinner for two."

"It sounds wonderful. But how would you feel
about making that a picnic dinner for *four*?"

Now it was Henry's turn to be puzzled. "Four?
I'm afraid I don't get it."

"Why, my twin sister. And I'm sure she'd like to
invite Bruce, a boy she met on the bus ride from the
airport."

"All right, then. Dinner for four it is."

While Susan and Henry made plans about where
and when to meet, as well as who would be
responsible for which part of their picnic dinner,
Chris was keeping busy, as well. She had noticed
that as the hundreds of tourists began collecting
their belongings and moving out of the theater,
there was enough chaos to give her a chance to do
some exploring. While two or three of the tour
guides were standing at the doors, bidding their
guests good-bye, the rest of them—including Jennifer Franklin—had retreated through a door on one
side of the theater. On it, Chris saw, there was a
sign that read "Employees Only."

After looking to the right, to the left, and behind
her, making sure that no one was watching her,
Chris placed her hand on the doorknob and turned it

slowly. As she'd expected, it wasn't locked. Holding her breath, she opened the door and slipped inside.

Since she'd been expecting the worst, she was relieved to discover that she'd stumbled into something that resembled a lounge. Gray metal lockers lined one wall, and vending machines with soda pop, candy bars, and snacks stood on the other. Near the door was a stack of freshly cleaned and pressed uniforms. The large room was L-shaped, and in the distant corner, just around the bend, Chris could see that there were tables and chairs set up. The tour guides, all of them dressed identically in their bright green outfits, were gathering there with brown-bag lunches and cans of cold soda pop.

With all the noise and confusion, no one seemed to notice her—something that was just fine with Chris.

I'll just file this little piece of information away, she was thinking. It might come in handy some time. But for now, I'd better get back to Susan, before she notices I'm gone. . . .

Just as she was about to leave, however, something out of ordinary suddenly caught Chris's attention. Amidst the noise of the happy chatter and merry laughter of the tour guides on their lunchbreak arose the sound of one angry voice, far louder than all the rest.

"If you think you're going to get away with this, Jennifer . . ." a deep male voice boomed.

"Please, Ricky," a female voice pleaded, "can't we go talk about this somewhere else?"

Chris ducked behind the lockers so she could get a better look at the scene that was unfolding here in the lunchroom—a scene that everyone was watching, their cheerful conversation having instantly faded into a strained silence. Sure enough, there was Jennifer, sitting at one of the tables with three or four other young women, all of them about ready to start eating their lunches. Beside her was a man about her age, sloppily dressed in jeans and a gray sweatshirt. He was grabbing her arm roughly, Chris was alarmed to see.

"Hey, let go of her," one of the other girls insisted, coming to the rescue of her friend.

"Yes, leave Jennifer alone, you big jerk," said one of the other girls sitting at the table.

"No, it's okay, really," Jennifer assured them in a meek voice. But the look of misery on her face gave out an entirely different message.

After casting a grateful look at her friends, Jennifer stood up from the table. She turned to the boy and said, "Let's go outside, Ricky. Please! We can talk about this there."

"You're right we're going to talk about this," Ricky returned, his dark eyes narrowed into tiny slits. "I'm getting pretty tired of you giving me such a hard time, Jennifer. You and I are going to settle this, once and for all!"

Jennifer looked so unhappy as she led this mean young man out of the lounge, through a back door that apparently led outside, that it was all Chris could do to keep from rushing over to her. Yet she knew that she was not here to offer sympathy or friendship—even to someone who looked as if she desperately needed it.

No, if she were going to help Jennifer Franklin, it had to be in some other way. Donald Franklin's hunch was right; there *was* something strange going on. And Chris was suddenly more determined than ever to find out exactly what it was.

Once again, she was about to retreat from the employees' lounge, to tell her sister about what she had seen, when she heard a startling conversation among Jennifer's friends.

"I don't know why Jennifer goes out with him," one of the young women exclaimed once Jennifer and Ricky had left the room, shutting the door behind them. Even so, from behind the closed door came the sounds of a heated argument, with Ricky yelling and Jennifer sounding as if she were on the verge of tears.

"Yes, it's hard to understand what on earth she sees in him," agreed one of the others. "They're both so different! Jennifer's so sweet and sincere, and that Ricky is so pushy and mean. . . ."

"And the way he treats her is just terrible," interrupted a third. "I don't get it at all."

So this awful young man, Ricky, really is Jennifer's new boyfriend, thought Chris, shocked. The one Mr. Franklin mentioned last night. But her girlfriends are right; why would she go out with someone who was obviously in the habit of treating her so poorly? It just doesn't make any sense!

By then, the noise level inside the employees' lounge had increased once again, so that it was impossible for Chris to overhear any more conversation. Besides, she had been away much longer than she had intended. The auditorium was probably empty by now, and Susan was no doubt worried sick. . . .

Sure enough; as Chris sneaked out of the lounge, back into the auditorium, she discovered that it was, indeed, empty, although the next group of tourists was already filing in. She hurried out the door, wondering how she'd ever manage to find her sister—and ran smack into Susan, standing there calmly, chatting with Henry Hartley.

"Oh, *there* you are!" said Susan, looking over at her twin and smiling innocently. "Did you find that bracelet you lost?"

"What bracelet? I just . . ." It took Chris a few seconds to figure out what her twin was talking about. And then she caught on. "Oh, yes. I got it. It's right here in my pocket. It was just as you said, Sooz. It had fallen off right outside that warehouse full of costumes. The catch is broken."

"Well, at least you got it back," Susan said. "By the way, Chris, Henry has volunteered to be our new guide of the city of Los Angeles. Tonight, he's taking us to the Hollywood Bowl for a concert. And that's not all. He's also offered to give us both a private demonstration of some of the special effects he's so interested in. You and I are really getting an 'insider's' look at Los Angeles—*and* the movie industry—aren't we?"

The threesome's conversation turned to a brief discussion of the city's most worthwhile sights, until Henry finally insisted that he had to get back to work. Once the twins were left alone, Susan turned to Chris.

"So, Ms. Super-sleuth, did you find out anything?"

Chris laughed. "Susan Pratt, how on earth did you know that's what I was doing?"

"What else would you be doing, sneaking away like that?"

"I wasn't *sneaking* exactly. . . . Well, maybe I was. . . ."

"Chris, what did you find out?" Susan demanded, suddenly impatient.

"Oh, Sooz, I found out something really strange!" Chris's voice had dropped down to a whisper. "I saw Jennifer and that new boyfriend of hers, the one Mr. Franklin mentioned. That Ricky Wheeler, remember? There's definitely something peculiar going on!"

She proceeded to tell her twin all about the scene she had witnessed in the employees' lounge, as well as the conversation among Jennifer's three girlfriends right afterward. Susan listened carefully to every single word.

"Wow!" she exclaimed once her sister was finished. "It sounds as if there really is something going on with Jennifer Franklin—and that this 'boyfriend' of hers has something to do with it."

"At least we have something to go on," said Chris. "I think we may as well head back to Aunt Karen's now, since I've already seen what I needed to see. The next thing for us to do is find out more about this Ricky, and why on earth Jennifer is interested in him."

"Yes," Susan agreed thoughtfully. "From what you've said, it sounds as if finding out more about Ricky Wheeler is going to be key in our investigation."

Both girls were silent as they headed back to the parking lot. It was Chris who finally spoke, but not until they were both seated inside their car.

"There's just one thing, Sooz." Her voice was a hoarse whisper. "I just hope this Ricky character isn't dangerous."

From the look on her sister's face as she glanced over at her, Chris could tell that her twin had just been thinking the exact same thing.

Five

When Bruce Jackson telephoned early the next morning with an invitation to spend the day sunning, swimming, and surfing on one of his favorite beaches, the twins agreed to postpone the Popcorn Project temporarily.

"After all," Chris reminded her twin with a teasing grin, "even the best sleuths need a break some time!"

When they returned to their aunt's apartment late that afternoon, they discovered that there was even more fun in store for them—and a kind of fun that they could combine with some investigating.

"Guess what!" cried Aunt Karen as Chris and Susan walked in the door, tired but exhilarated from their full day of enjoying one of California's most famous attractions. "You two have been invited to a party."

"A party! How exciting!" cried Susan.

"When is it?" Chris wanted to know.

"It's tonight," Karen replied.

"Who's giving it?" asked Susan. Already she and her sister were peeling off the damp shirts they had thrown over their bathing suits as they got ready to jump into the shower.

"Why, your newest friend here in Los Angeles. None other than Donald Franklin."

Susan and Chris were both caught off guard. For the time being, they had both forgotten all about the Popcorn Project—and the plight of Donald Franklin and his daughter. Even so, this was a nice surprise.

"What's the occasion?" asked Chris.

"I'm not sure, exactly. But when he telephoned earlier today to invite your both, he said something about wanting to give you two a chance to meet some of Jennifer's friends."

The twins exchanged glances.

"My goodness, he certainly is giving the two of us the royal treatment," said Susan.

"Or else he's just looking for nice things to do for his daughter. At any rate, maybe we can find out more about Jennifer tonight. And," she added with a twinkle in her brown eyes, "have a lot of fun in the process."

The party at Donald Franklin's house was nothing short of spectacular. Tonight, there were strings of white light illuminating the entire area around the pool, including the large patio on which the twins had had dinner with Donald and Jennifer. A small chamber orchestra played in the background, with violins, flutes and a harp serenading the guests with lovely melodies. A large table, covered with a pale pink linen tablecloth, lined one side of the pool. On it was a sumptuous buffet of food.

As the guests, the twins estimated that there were at least sixty beautifully dressed people milling around the pool area, tasting the delicious food as they chatted in small groups. There were people of all ages, some obviously Jennifer's friends, some Mr. Franklin's.

The twins took full advantage of this setting to talk to as many people as they could, all with an ear toward finding out more about Jennifer Franklin— and Ricky Wheeler. No matter whom they talked to, everyone came up with the same conclusion: that Jennifer was an honest, caring person who was incapable of hurting anybody. As for Ricky, most of Jennifer's friends had never even heard of him. And those who had, had absolutely nothing good to say about him.

Finally, Susan caught Chris's eye and gave her a look that could only mean one thing: that it was time for a powwow.

"What's up, Sooz?" asked Chris, wandering over to her sister. "Finding out anything helpful?"

"Well, to tell you the truth . . . Here, why don't you and I take a little walk? That way, we can talk without the danger of anyone overhearing us."

Arm and arm, the two girls began strolling away from the pool area, out to the lovely manicured gardens and grounds surrounding the Franklin home. They followed a narrow winding path that led through lush flowering bushes and trees, vibrant pinks and reds and oranges that were colorful backdrops for the dramatic palm trees that also dotted the property. And then, once they felt they were far enough away from the others not to be overheard, Susan began to speak earnestly.

"It's this whole thing with Jennifer, Chris. Something is definitely wrong. Look, everything we've been able to find out about her tells us the same thing: that's she's a lovely, sweet girl who never did anything to hurt anybody in her entire life! Yet here she is, acting so strange all of a sudden . . . just like her father said."

"Yes, I know. And that's only the beginning." With a loud sigh, Chris dropped onto a charming concrete bench with ornately carved legs, placed alongside the path, right underneath a fragrant flowering tree with bright pink blossoms. "Then there's that Ricky Wheeler. Talk about bad news!"

"It doesn't seem to make any sense, does it?" Susan sat down next to her twin. "He's such a bad egg. Not the kind of person I'd expect Jennifer to want to associate with at all."

Chris frowned. "Well, as far as I'm concerned, it all adds up to one thing. There's something very fishy going on between Jennifer and Ricky."

"What do you mean, 'fishy'?" asked Susan.

"I think this 'romance' of theirs isn't really a romance at all. Sure, they're *associated* with each other in some way—some *bad* way, I suspect. But I'm not so sure they're actually going out."

Susan was surprised. "But what about those three girlfriends of Jennifer's? You know, the ones you overheard talking at the employees' lounge yesterday? They seemed convinced that Ricky is Jennifer's boyfriend, and they should know."

"Yes, but maybe they just believe that because Jennifer *wants* people to believe that!"

Susan shook her head. "Wait a minute, Chris. Now I'm *totally* confused. Why would Jennifer want people to believe something like that if it wasn't true? Especially since the person in question is that awful boy Ricky?"

"That, I don't know." Chris rested her chin in her hands. "You know, Sooz, I feel that in the last thirty-six hours, you and I have found out a lot about Jennifer Franklin. But do you know what's totally frustrating? None of it seems to make a bit of sense!"

"Well, then," burst out another voice, totally unexpectedly, "maybe that means you two should just leave me alone and start minding your own business!"

Both Chris and Susan were so startled that they jumped. Chris, in fact, almost fell off the bench.

"What . . . who . . . ?"

The twins looked around and saw that directly behind them, on the other side of the huge tree, densely covered with its late summer blossoms, there was a small green shed, probably for gardening tools. In fact, as the heavy wooden door was pushed open and the red-faced Jennifer Franklin emerged, her blue eyes flashing with anger, a rake nearly came toppling out.

"Jennifer!" Susan cried. "What were you *doing* in there?"

With furious jerking motions, Jennifer tried to wipe away the tears that were streaming down her cheeks. "Having a good cry, if you want to know the truth!"

"Why?" asked Chris, torn between confusion and concern.

"That's none of your business!" Jennifer snapped. "And I'll tell you two busybodies something else, too. Everything else about my life is none of your business, either! Not my friends, not Ricky . . . none of it! So why don't you just find something else to do besides *bothering* people while you're on your California vacation?"

Susan and Chris glanced at each other in amazement. This was one of the few times in the twins' lives that neither one of them could think of a thing to say.

But Jennifer's next comment changed all that.

"And here I thought you two were nice!" she went on. "I even thought that maybe we could be friends! Instead I find out that you've been *spying* on me . . . !"

"Now, wait a minute!" Chris protested. "We were only trying to help."

"Oh, really?" Jennifer retorted. "And why are you so interested in helping me?"

"Actually," Chris said calmly, "it's your father we were most interested in helping."

Instantly Jennifer froze. And the look in her eyes suddenly changed from anger to shock.

"My father!" she repeated, her voice nearly a whisper. "What does *he* have to do with any of this?"

"Not much . . . except for the fact that he happens to be very concerned about you, Jennifer. He loves you, and he's worried sick about you. And he told us that he suspects that that creepy boyfriend of yours, Ricky, has something to do with whatever it is that's been bothering you lately. . . ."

"Chris!" Susan grabbed hold of her sister's arm. "Please, just let it go, will you? Maybe Jennifer's right. Maybe none of this *is* any of our business!"

"But it *is* Mr. Franklin's business," Chris insisted, her eyes still fixed on the tearful Jennifer. "He's so upset, and we made a vow to try and help him."

"Chris, let's just get out of here. Please!"

Chris took a deep breath. "Okay. Let's go back to the party, Sooz. You know, Jennifer, when I first met you, I thought you were nice, too. But then I found out that you're doing all these things to hurt your father. Closing him out of your life, refusing to talk to him . . . not even introducing him to this new boyfriend of yours. Well, to tell you the truth, I'm not so sure any more that you *are* so nice!"

With that, she turned on her heel, stalking back to the pool area where the party was still in full swing. Susan scrambled after her, after casting one more sympathetic look back at Jennifer and seeing that the look on her face was one of true anguish.

"Christine Pratt, what on earth got *into* you?"

Susan demanded once they were halfway back to the pool. "You really lit into poor Jennifer back there!"

"Oh, it was all an act," Chris grumbled. "One that didn't work the way I'd hoped it would," she added grimly.

"It was an *act*? You mean you weren't really so furious with Jennifer?"

"No, not at all. Why should I be? I just hoped that since she'd overheard us and found out we'd been trying to find out what was making her act so strange lately *anyway*, maybe hearing about the effect that all her mysterious behavior was having on her father might make her come to her senses. But as you saw yourself," Chris concluded with a shrug, "it didn't work."

Susan stopped a few feet before the two steps that led up to the pool area and sighed. "So, now what? We can't keep following Jennifer around, because she's on to us. And she's not about to tell us anything, either. I think that's pretty obvious. No, I'd say that as of right now, the Popcorn Project is officially *off*. That is, unless you've got an idea . . . ?"

Hopefully Susan glanced over at her sister. But Chris just shook her head slowly.

"Nope," she said sadly. "I'm afraid that, this time, I haven't got a single idea."

The next morning, the feeling of gloom that had descended over both twins as a result of their botched attempt at investigating Jennifer Franklin's sudden change in behavior continued to hang over them. They sat in silence over their breakfast, not even touching their fresh-squeezed orange juice or the large plate of scrambled eggs that Chris had just made.

"Cheer up, you two," Aunt Karen said brightly. "You tried your best. So what if it didn't work out? Besides, this is supposed to be a *vacation*, remember? Now that you're free of your sleuthing responsibilities, you'll have more time for *fun*."

Before Chris had a chance to explain that, to her and her sister, sleuthing *was* fun, there was a soft *thump* outside the front door.

"What's that?" Susan asked, startled.

"Oh, it sounds like the newspaper was just delivered." Without very much enthusiasm, Chris dragged herself out of her kitchen chair. "I'll get it."

Karen looked up with surprise. "It's a bit early for the newspaper," she commented.

"Hey, you're right," Chris called over from the front door. "It's not the newspaper."

Karen and Susan watched from the kitchen as she crouched down in the doorway and picked up a shoebox-sized package. She brought it back to the table immediately. The parcel was wrapped in heavy brown paper, but it hadn't been sent through the mail. In fact, the only markings on the outside were the twins' names, Susan and Christine Pratt, printed neatly in black magic marker.

"What on earth . . . ?" muttered Chris, placing the mysterious box smack in the middle of the kitchen table, then sitting down in front of it.

"Well, you know what they say," her twin retorted. "There's only one way to find out!"

Eagerly, Susan tore into the box, ripping off the brown paper and discovering that there was, indeed, a shoe box inside.

"Maybe some secret admirer is sending you girls presents," Aunt Karen suggested, looking on with great curiosity.

"Or maybe some secret admirer has decided that it's high time Sooz and I started wearing better-looking shoes," Chris joked.

Despite their kidding, however, all three of them were anxious—and a little bit apprehensive. After all, this package had certainly arrived in a peculiar way, as if its sender wanted his or her identity to remain a secret.

So Chris was just a little bit nervous as she lifted off the cover, half expecting something to jump out at her.

She was surprised, then, and maybe even a little bit disappointed, when she opened up the box and found that it was practically empty. The only thing inside was a small piece of paper, folded twice.

"What is it, Chris?" Susan demanded eagerly.

Her sister frowned. "I'm not sure, Sooz. It looks like a letter or something. . . ." Carefully she unfolded it, anxious to figure out what this was all about.

"Why, it looks like a clipping from a magazine or a newspaper." Aunt Karen peered over at the slick piece of paper in her niece's hand, on which, she could see, was printed a short article.

"You're right, Aunt Karen." Chris glanced at the bottom of the page and recognized the name of a trade magazine for the motion picture industry, the kind of publication that is read mainly by people who work for movie studios. The date that this particular issue of the magazine had been published was also printed there: June 21.

"This article came out a little less than two months ago." Chris still couldn't figure out what this was all about.

"What does it say?" Without waiting for an answer, Susan came around to Chris's side of the table and, looking over her shoulder, began to read.

Instead of finally understanding what this strange "gift" was all about, however, both Chris and Susan only became even more confused as they simultaneously read the article.

Finally, Aunt Karen could no longer stand the suspense. "What does it say, girls? Is it from Jennifer Franklin, by any chance?"

"I really don't know," Susan replied. "I guess it could be. But if it is, I'm afraid I don't understand what it could possibly have to do with her."

"Me, either," Chris agreed. "It's an article about Silver Screen Studios—but that's where any possible tie to Jennifer ends. All it says is that Silver Screen is currently in the process of developing some really innovative special effects for a blockbuster science-fiction movie. According to this, they're planning to start filming in the late summer or early autumn. Apparently the studio is being quite secretive about it. . . ." She let her sentence trail off, wishing that somehow its meaning would snap into place, but frustrated by the realization that it wasn't about to.

"It *must* be from Jennifer," Susan said, shaking her head slowly. "Who else could have sent it?"

"How about her father?" suggested Aunt Karen.

The twins glanced at each other.

"I doubt it," said Susan.

"There'd be no reason for him to be sending us mysterious packages," Chris agreed. "No, I'm with Sooz on this one. It's *got* to be from Jennifer. The question is, *why*?"

"Maybe she thought about it all last night and decided that she wants us to help her after all," Susan mused.

"Then why is she being so mysterious?" Chris countered. "She could have just called us up and *told* us, for heaven's sake!"

Chris looked at her twin, hoping for an answer to her question. Instead, she saw on her sister's face the same confusion that she herself was feeling.

"I don't know," Susan said softly. "But do you know what I think?"

"What?"

"I think that Jennifer—or whoever it is who sent us this article—wants us to find out!"

Chris thought for a minute, and then her brown eyes began to gleam. "You know, you're right. And do you know what that means?"

Susan nodded. "The Pratt sisters are back in the sleuthing business once again."

"That's right," cried Chris. "The Popcorn Project is on, full speed ahead!"

Six

"*Sooz, I think this was a real brainstorm,*" said Chris. "Following Ricky Wheeler around, to see what he's up to. . . . Why, that was true inspiration."

"Maybe so," said Susan modestly. "That still remains to be seen. Before we decide how much of a 'brainstorm' it was, let's see if we actually find *out* anything."

The mysterious "clue" that had been sent anonymously that morning had made the twins more enthusiastic about the Popcorn Project than ever. In fact, they had decided not to waste a single minute more. After gulping down their breakfast, they had rushed over to the Los Angeles telephone book to look up Ricky Wheeler's address. Then, they climbed into their aunt's car and drove over to his apartment building.

Now, they were sitting outside, parked right across the street. Both of them were wearing disguises of sunglasses and big hats that Aunt Karen had lent them. On the seat, in between them, was a pair of binoculars.

"Well, we're bound to find out at least *something* about Ricky Wheeler," said Chris. "And I, for one, am still convinced that he's behind Jennifer Franklin's 'mysterious' behavior."

"I just hope we haven't missed him." Susan was beginning to sound woeful. "It's already past nine."

But before long, she sensed that her sister had suddenly grown tense.

"There he is, Sooz." Chris's voice was almost a whisper. "At least I think that's him. . . ." She reached for the binoculars, slouched down in the front seat, and then peered at the man leaving the apartment building across the street.

"That's Ricky Wheeler, all right. I'm positive."

"Great! What do we do now?"

"We follow him, of course."

Without waiting another second, Susan turned the key in the ignition. Then, as if to lessen some of the tension that was already filling the car, she turned to her twin and said, "I guess this is it, Chris. As they say in the movies, 'The chase is on!' "

The twins were actually laughing as they drove off slowly, with Susan taking care to stay a safe distance away from Ricky's car, at least two hundred feet behind. Traffic in this residential part of town was light, and following him was no problem. When he got onto the freeway, however, and began speeding along in the fast lane, the adventurousness of what they were doing struck the girls for the first time.

"Hold on to your hat, Chris!" Susan cried. "I'm going to have to do some fancy footwork here, if I'm going to keep up with Ricky!"

"Gee, this really *is* like a movie!" Despite her growing excitement, however, the slight waver in Chris's voice betrayed the fact that she was just a little bit nervous.

"There *is* one small difference," her twin replied, her hands gripping the steering wheel tightly and her eyes fixed on the road as she kept her foot pressed down hard on the accelerator even as she slid into another lane. "In the movies, there never seem to be any traffic cops around!"

Despite Susan's concern, the girls managed to keep pace with Ricky without any problem as he continued along the freeway for a few more miles. Even so, they were more than a little bit relieved when he eased off onto an exit ramp and they were able to slow down. They followed him through some local traffic, past gas stations and restaurants. Then he made a right turn and headed down a long road.

The twins' excitement—and their nervousness—grew with every block, every mile they traveled. And so they were actually disappointed when he turned again and drove into a parking lot—one that turned out to be a back entrance to Silver Screen Studios.

"Oh, no!" groaned Chris. "We're back here again! *Now* what?"

Her sister was equally deflated. "I'm afraid we have hit kind of a dead end. He's probably just visiting Jennifer again."

"Huh! 'Visiting?' " Chris snorted. "I'd say 'bothering' was more like it!"

"Either way, I can't imagine that there's anything for us to gain by following him into Silver Screen Studios. After all, you already had a chance to watch him in action the day before yesterday."

"Yes," Chris agreed with a sigh. "We might as well go back home and— Hey, wait a minute!"

"What is it?" Susan could tell by her sister's tone of voice that she had come up with a way out of this "dead end."

"So what if Ricky just stopped off here to see Jennifer? We can still hang around and follow him when he's done here, to find out what else Ricky Wheeler does with his time!"

"Chris, you're a genius! Boy, out of everybody in the world, I sure am glad I chose *you* to be my twin sister!"

"Thanks," Chris returned, grinning. "I'm honored."

It wasn't long before Chris's brainstorm paid off. After the girls had been sitting in the car in the Silver Screen Studios parking lot for less than half an hour, Susan nudged her sister.

"Here he comes again," she breathed. Once again, she started up the car, with the same determination as before. "Fasten your seat belts, ladies and gentlemen. It's time for 'take two' of the car chase!"

This time, their car ride lead them to a different part of town. Here, the endless squared-off blocks they traveled brought them through an area of run-down buildings and ugly warehouses. There were few cars on the road besides theirs and Ricky's. Both Chris and Susan began to grow a bit uncomfortable as they noticed the change in their surroundings. Even so, Susan continued to follow Ricky's car doggedly, being careful to stay even further behind than before so that he wouldn't notice he was being followed.

"Gosh, where do you think he's going?" Susan gulped.

"You know what they say, Sooz," Chris returned with forced gaiety. "There's only one way to find out!"

It wasn't long before that riddle was solved. Ricky's car slowed down in front of a large but seedy-looking group of buildings, all of them surrounded by a high chain-link fence. On the front gate was a large hand-lettered sign with peeling paint.

"There's the answer to our question," said Susan, pulling up alongside the curb half a block up from the building complex's main entrance. " 'Hollywood Productions.' "

"What's that?" Chris blinked. "Another movie studio?"

"That's what it looks like. Although this one looks as if it's not doing *quite* as well as Silver Screen Studios!"

"*That's* an understatement. So this is where Ricky was headed first thing after stopping off to see Jennifer at work. But what does it all mean?"

Susan shook her head slowly. "I haven't got the slightest idea, Chris. But one thing's for certain: I sure would love to find out!"

"Not much of a chance of that. Not with that huge fence all around, and the guard at the gate." Chris thought for a few seconds. "Do you think he works here?"

"From the way he was dressed, I'd say he hardly looked as if he were on his way to work! That is, unless he's an 'extra' in some movie they're making! You know, one of those characters in a movie who's in the background, but never says anything. . . ."

Chris snapped her fingers. "That's it! Sooz, you're a genius!"

"What on earth are you talking about, Chris?"

"That's how we can sneak inside and find out what Ricky's doing in there! Whether he works there . . . or what!"

"I'm afraid I still don't get it."

"Sooz, you and I will pass ourselves off as extras! We'll get into Hollywood Productions that way, and then we'll be able to have a look around. With a little luck," she went on, "we'll be able to see firsthand what Ricky Wheeler is doing behind those locked gates."

"Do you know what, Chris?" said Susan.

"No, what?"

"*You're* the one who's the genius! Come on, let's go."

"Wait a minute! If you and I are going to pretend we're here for the filming of a movie, shouldn't we have costumes or something?"

"I don't think so, Chris. If we really were extras in a film, the wardrobe department would provide them, don't you think? No, I'm afraid that this time, you and I are going to have to rely on nothing more than our acting ability."

"*And* our sheer nerve!" Chris joked with a nervous laugh.

With their heads held high, Susan and Chris drove their car up to the gate. Just as they'd expected, the guard came out and nodded at them.

"Can I help you girls?" he asked congenially. "You know, we don't give tours here. . . ."

"Oh, we're not tourists," Chris insisted, leaning over across the front seat. "We're extras. We're here to report for work."

"Extras, huh?" Frowning, the guard checked the clipboard he was carrying. "As far as I can see, the only movie being filmed today is *Creatures from the Planet Zoon*."

"That's it!" Susan cried. "We're the creatures! Well, two of them, anyway. They put all this makeup on us to make us look really scarey. I get a green nose, and my friend here gets pink hair and these really big horns. . . ."

The guard just scowled. "Now look, you two. This is no place for clowning around. I can't let just anybody in here. I don't believe for a minute that you two are in this movie or any other movie. . . ."

Susan cast her sister a rueful look, one that said they were about to lose this round. But the gleam in Chris's eye told her that she wasn't yet ready to give up.

"You're right," Chris told the guard calmly. "We're not extras, and we're not here to make a movie. We're here because we're friends of Ricky Wheeler, and we've got an appointment with some important people here at Hollywood Productions."

"Oh! Well!" Immediately the expression on the guard's face changed. "Friends of Ricky's, are you? He's got special permission from the *president* of Hollywood Productions to come and go as he pleases. If you're with him, then by all means come right in."

With that, he moved aside, then raised the barrier that had been preventing them from driving into the parking lot. Susan cast her twin a look of astonishment, then drove right in.

"Gee, Chris!" she said once they were out of earshot. "You sure said the magic word!"

Chris cast her a rueful grin. "Faking it in front of the guard was one thing. Now, you and I have got to take on all of Hollywood Productions!"

Fortunately, it appeared that there were actually very few people around. And those who were barely gave Chris and Susan a second glance.

"Where should we go?" Susan stood at the edge of a small courtyard—really, a sandy area covered with weeds—that led to the entrance of three different buildings.

"Oh, don't worry," Chris assured her. "I've got a foolproof way of making decisions like this."

"Really? What's that?"

Chris took a deep breath. "Eenie, meenie, miney, moe. . . ."

"Come on, you!" cried Susan, laughing. "Let's try this one first. Look, the worst thing that can happen is that we get thrown out of here, right?"

"Sure, Sooz," Chris gulped. "That is, I *hope* that's the worst thing. . . ."

Almost as soon as they opened the door of the first building, the one immediately to their left, the twins slammed it shut once again. Inside was a real movie set—lights, cameras, actors, scenery, everything. And, just as the guard had said, it looked as if they were indeed filming a science-fiction movie. Grotesque-looking creatures, orange and green with elephantlike trunks and large horns, were circling a spaceship that looked as if it were made out of cardboard and aluminum foil.

"Hey, did you check out those guys from the Planet Zoon?" joked Chris as she and her sister made their hasty exit. "I wasn't far off when I started describing them to that guard."

"See that? Maybe you should forget about a career in law and instead become a costume designer!"

The second building, the one on the girls' right, had considerably less going on inside. Even so, both girls jumped as they opened the front door and found themselves face to face with a huge ugly monster, baring his sharp teeth.

"Whoa!" Chris gasped. "What on earth . . . ?"

"Relax, Chris. It's just a warehouse. See? It's

full of costumes and sets and props, ones just like that friendly gentleman over by the door who greeted us with such a big smile as we came in."

Chris shivered as she looked around. "I don't know, Sooz. This place gives me the creeps."

Slowly, cautiously, the two girls made their way through the dark, shadowy space, past rows of chairs in every style imaginable, around racks of Civil War–style dresses, among shelves containing everything from lamps and telephones to shoes and old-fashioned bonnets complete with satin ribbons and long dramatic plumes.

Susan, too, was finding it kind of spooky, being in here, wandering through the shadows among such a strange combination of things. In fact, she was about to suggest that she and Chris get out when she heard someone talking in a low voice.

"Sh-h-h!" Her voice had dropped to a low whisper. "Duck down, Chris. Come back in here. I think I heard something. . . ."

Sure enough; as the twins crouched down behind a row of fake trees and bushes, then crept stealthily toward the sound of voices, they came across a back corner of the warehouse where three people, two men and a woman, were carefully studying a television screen. It was an odd sight, in a place like this. But that was precisely what was making the twins so curious.

"Run that section of tape over again," said one of the men, his back to the girls' hiding place. "I think I'm beginning to get an idea of how that laser effect works."

"Sure enough, Jay." The other man pressed a few buttons on what looked like a VCR. The three people watched attentively as on the screen, a person dressed in a futuristic outfit shot a weapon that gave off an incredibly blinding light. It was an impressive sight—a fact that wasn't wasted on any of them.

"Wow! Those people over at Silver Screen Studios sure know their stuff" the woman exclaimed. "This is fantastic!"

"Yeah, I'll say," said one of the men. "But don't worry. I bet with a little bit of fooling around on the computer, we can duplicate it without any problem. Hey, I just had an idea. . . ."

"Not yet," said the first man. "Let's watch the entire cassette before we start trying to copy these effects."

"Well, all right, but we'd better get moving," the woman insisted. "Didn't the boss say that Wheeler was bringing over another cassette today?"

One of the men let out a low whistle. "Boy, that Wheeler sure is a smooth operator! I've got to give him a lot of credit. But, here, let's go back and see that segment with the laser gun again. . . ."

At that point, Susan tugged at Chris's skirt, and the two girls slunk away, back toward the door of the warehouse. For now, they had seen enough.

"Gosh, did you see what they were doing, Sooz?" Chris cried once they were outside again. "They're looking at video cassettes showing special effects—cassettes that were stolen from Silver Screen Studios—and copying them!"

"That's certainly how it looks," Susan agreed. "And it's just like it said in that magazine article that arrived on our doorstep so mysteriously. They're specially developed high-tech effects created for the new movie Silver Screen Studios is filming right about now."

"Yes, and Ricky Wheeler's the one who's been sneaking them out."

Suddenly, the twins looked at each other in horror.

"Sooz, are you thinking what I'm thinking?" Chris asked slowly.

"I am if what you're thinking is that Jennifer's the one who's been stealing the cassettes, and then handing them over to Ricky."

Chris nodded. "I'm afraid that that's exactly what I was thinking. Oh, Sooz!" she wailed. "I can't believe that Jennifer's involved in something illegal. Imagine, stealing secrets from the movie studio where she works . . . as well as the place where her father works. Gee, I don't want to believe that it's true."

"It is hard to believe," Susan agreed. "But you've got to admit, it does look as if that's precisely what's going on."

"Well, we don't have any proof, at least not yet. . . ."

By now, Chris actually felt dizzy. Was it really possible that Jennifer was capable of doing something like this? More important, why on earth would someone like her ever get involved in such a terrible thing? Surely Ricky was behind it . . .

even so, it was difficult to imagine that Jennifer would ever consent to cooperate.

"Well, I guess there's no reason why we should stop now," Susan was saying. "We've already checked out two of the three buildings, so we might as well see what's inside the third."

"I'm almost afraid to," said Chris. "The more we find out, the more I wish we'd never even gotten involved in any of this." Even so, she followed her twin into the third building.

Inside there were offices, all of them leading off a long hallway so that no one saw the girls come in. Many of them were empty, in fact, and in the few that were occupied, people were busy typing or talking on the telephone. Susan and Chris slipped through the building with ease, stopping periodically to listen to snippets of conversations. But nothing was of very great interest.

That is, until they heard Ricky Wheeler's loud voice, booming from behind a partially closed door. The twins stood outside, able to listen in without being seen.

"Yeah, this whole thing has been no sweat," Ricky was bragging. "All it takes is having the right connections on the inside. And I'm telling you, the girl who's been helping me out has got connections pretty high up."

"Listen, Ricky," another voice interrupted, "I've told you all along, I'm not interested in knowing who's been smuggling these cassette tapes out of Silver Screen Studios. That's your concern, not ours. Just deliver the goods, and you'll get your money."

"Sure." Ricky laughed coldly. "And the money's great. Now, here's the latest tape. I just picked it up this morning. I just hope you've got the money you owe me. . . ."

"Don't worry." The man who was speaking was beginning to sound a little bit irritated. "I've got your money right here, in this envelope."

"Great. Nothing like dealing with the people at the top. Thanks a lot. And don't forget, as long as you keep on holding up your end of the deal, there's more where that came from."

There were sounds of people pushing back chairs and standing up, and Chris and Susan could tell that the meeting between Ricky Wheeler and the man they assumed was the president of Hollywood Productions was over. They scurried down the hall and out the building, then dashed back to their car.

By the time Susan started it up and was heading out of the parking lot, Chris was practically in tears.

"It's true!" she cried. "Jennifer *is* stealing those video cassette tapes and giving them to Ricky. And he's selling them to one of Silver Screen Studio's competitors. Right now, those three people in the warehouse are trying their hardest to copy them. Oh, Sooz, I don't want to believe that Jennifer is involved in all this."

"Neither do I, Chris," Susan said, shaking her head sadly. "But you've got to admit that it certainly looks that way."

Neither of the twins did very much talking after that. As they drove back to their aunt's apartment, they were too busy thinking about Jennifer and

Ricky and the illegal dealing the two were involved in.

More than that, they were thinking about the fact that it was up to them to decide whether or not to tell Donald Franklin that his daughter was stealing secrets from the place where he worked, a movie studio that was about to honor him for twenty-five years of loyal service.

Seven

That afternoon, the girls found themselves putting the Popcorn Project on hold for a second time— once again because of a most welcome distraction. Henry Hartley had arranged to show Susan and Chris the technology behind the authentic-looking masks that they had seen at Silver Screen Studios' special effects demonstration.

"Where are we going, anyway?" asked Susan as she and her twin followed Henry into one of the buildings that hadn't been a part of their tour a few days earlier.

"The special-effects laboratory is in one of the older buildings, one that used to be used for filming movies but which has more or less been abandoned. Studio B, they call it. It's funny; it's still set up from the last movie they made there. One of those jungle films. You know the type: lots of guys with

English accents running around in khaki shorts and pith helmets."

"Sure, I've seen those on TV on Sunday afternoons," Chris said with a grin. "They're always hunting elephants and lions."

"Well, not in this one. From what I understand, this one was about a bunch of people trying to trap jungle animals to bring them back home to put in a zoo. Hey, are you interested in seeing the set?"

"You bet!" Chris cried.

Studio B looked exactly the way the girls imagined it would. It contained cameras, lights, and all kinds of other equipment, just like the other sets they had seen on the studio tour. But here, the scenery recreated a jungle scene. There was thick vegetation everywhere, exotic flowering bushes, palm trees and long dramatic vines, and on the floor was soft fake grass, forming a small hill. But the best part was a rickety bridge hanging overhead, made of rough-hewn rope and wooden slats.

"This is fantastic!" Chris said. "Just like every jungle movie I've ever seen."

"Yeah," Henry agreed. "Too bad nobody uses it anymore." He shrugged. "I guess that kind of movie has gone out of style, anyway.

"But enough of this. How about heading over to the special-effects lab now?"

"Are you sure it's okay?" asked Susan as she and her twin accompanied Henry into another part of the same building.

"No problem," Henry assured them. "Max, who's in charge here is not only one of the best technicians in the business; he also happens to be a good buddy of mine. In fact, we have kind of a deal going."

The twins exchanged alarmed glances.

"Deal?" Chris blinked. "What kind of deal?"

"I promise to keep him posted on all the newest techniques I learn in school, and he lets me play around in here any time I want."

"Oh, I see." Susan was more than a little relieved.

"In fact, here he is now. Hi, there, Max. Is it okay if I show two friends of mine some of the ropes?"

The plump, balding man they passed in the hall simply glanced at them, then turned his attention to Henry, smiling at him over thick glasses. "Sure, Henry. Make yourself at home. Just be careful in there."

"Okay, then." Proudly Henry opened a door, and the threesome stepped into the spacious room that housed the special-effects laboratory. "Let me show you how some of that famous 'Hollywood magic' is created!"

For the next few hours, Henry showed the girls, step by step, the process used in making the latex masks that could be used to create any kind of face—including the exact replica of a real person. He used Chris as the model as Susan watched in fascination. First, he made a plaster cast of her face, one that was identical in every way simply because he had used her face itself to make the mold. Then, once the plaster had hardened, he stretched a soft piece of rubber over it, duplicating her features with perfect accuracy.

"It looks just like me!" Chris cried, viewing the mask for the first time.

"That's funny," teased Susan. "I was just about to say that it looks exactly like *me*."

"Well, the truth is, it doesn't look exactly like either of you," Henry said. "At least, not yet. This silhouette still needs to be painted, in order to create natural-looking skin tones and little details like freckles or beauty marks."

Another thought occurred to Susan. "What about eye color?"

"Easy. See that cabinet over there?" He gestured toward a metal cabinet, placed up on the wall. "Inside are contact lenses of every color imaginable. And in that cabinet, there are all kinds of wigs. See?" he added with a grin. "We've thought of everything!"

As they left the studio late that afternoon, they were still overwhelmed by the authenticity of the mask they were carrying home with them to show their aunt. Even more than that, Susan was thrilled that she had had a chance to learn about a brand new kind of "art."

"Gee, that was really something, wasn't it?" she said with a sigh. "Henry's quite a good painter. He managed to recreate every little detail of your face with amazing skill."

"Maybe you'll have to try your hand at mask-making one of these days, Sooz," Chris said. "After all, you're pretty handy with a paint brush."

"No, thanks. I think that, for now, I'll just stick to painting on paper."

When they returned to Aunt Karen's, they eagerly told her all about the special-effects demonstration Henry had given them, then busied themselves doing some errands for her. Aside from the fact that they were beginning to feel as if they had been neglecting their poor, incapacitated relative, they wanted a chance to step back from the excitement of sightseeing in order to think objectively about the Popcorn Project—in particular, its latest development.

As far as they were concerned, the very worst thing that could happen *had* happened. They had found out that Jennifer Franklin was involved in something terrible—something that was guaranteed to hurt her father very, very much.

"I'm still not sure I believe it," Susan said thoughtfully as she folded the clean clothes she had just taken out of one of the dryers in the apartment building's laundry room.

"That's because you don't *want* to believe it. To tell you the truth, Sooz, I feel exactly the same way." Chris glanced up from the avocados she was slicing for the salad portion of that evening's dinner. "But the real question is, Do we tell Mr. Franklin what we found out about his daughter?"

Susan sighed. "I don't know, Chris. Look, why don't we forget about it for now, and instead concentrate on getting dinner ready? We'd better start the chicken. . . . What time is it, anyway?"

Automatically Chris glanced down at her wrist—then felt a twinge of despair.

"Hey, Sooz?" she said mournfully. "Remember when we were at Silver Screen Studios the first time, and we pretended that I'd lost a bracelet in order to create a cover story for my absence?"

"Yes. . . ."

"Well, now I'm afraid I've lost my watch. Only this time, it's for real."

"Oh, no! Not your brand new watch, the one that was a graduation present from Mom and Dad. Do you have any idea where . . ."

"*I* know!" Chris snapped her fingers. "I must have left it at the Franklins', the evening we went swimming in their pool. I'll bet anything it's on the floor of the cabana I used to change my clothes."

"Well, then, why don't we stop over there and see? The sooner, the better. If you don't mind me making a pun, let's not waste any *time*. . . ."

Chris groaned loudly, then burst out laughing. Sure enough, when the girls called the Franklins' house, the housekeeper who answered said she had, indeed, found a watch fitting Chris's description, right on the floor of one of the poolside cabanas. She told them that they were welcome to drop by any time to pick it up.

It wasn't long before the twins drove up to the Beverly Hills mansion, eager to retrieve Chris's lost property. The housekeeper let them in, gave them the watch, and then invited them to help themselves to some lemonade in the kitchen while she finished dusting the bedrooms upstairs.

"Wow, that was lucky," Chris commented as she took a big gulp of lemonade, then leaned against one of the tall wooden stools in the kitchen. "I'm glad I got my lost watch back so easily."

But before Susan had a chance to reply, the twins suddenly heard loud voices coming from the next room—a study, from what they could recall from their other visits to the Franklins' home. Actually, it wasn't very difficult to hear everything that was being said, since the two rooms were separated by slatted wooden doors that opened up above one of the counters, into the study, to form a pass-through.

"I thought I told you never to come here!" Jennifer was saying.

"Hey, hey," a male voice jeered. "I figured you'd be as pleased as punch to see me."

The twins glanced at each other, then pressed their faces up against the slatted wooden doors. Through the narrow openings, it was easy to watch the scene that was unfolding in the next room. Sure enough, there was Jennifer. And the young man she was arguing with was none other than Ricky Wheeler.

"Let's get one thing straight, Ricky," she told him firmly. "It may be true that I've agreed to enter into a . . . shall we say, a 'business relationship' with you. But don't believe, even for a second, that that means I'll *ever* be 'happy' to see you."

Instead of being angry, Ricky just laughed a cold, mean laugh. "Aw, you're just a little bit stuck-up, that's all. Sooner or later, you'll come around." He strutted over to Jennifer and slung his arm around her waist.

She, however, stepped away from him neatly,

then looked at him through eyes burning with anger. "Do you think I could ever be interested in a *blackmailer*?"

"Hey, don't be so rough on me," Ricky retorted, laughing again in that same ugly way. "I'm basically a nice guy, you know. Even you thought so, those first two or three times we went out together. Calling me a blackmailer isn't being fair. I'm just your average guy, trying to make a living."

"Oh, really? Do you think that 'average guys' make their living by stealing video cassettes of newly developed special effects from one movie studio, then selling them to another?"

"Wait a minute, sweetie. *I'm* not the one stealing them; *you* are, remember? Yes," he went on, folding his arms across his chest and smiling smugly, "between that little job of yours, giving tours at Silver Screen Studios, and the fact that you know your way around your daddy's office pretty well, things have worked out great, haven't they? It gives you a chance to get a hold of those valuable cassettes showing those secret special effects and hand them over to me—without anybody ever being the wiser."

"You're hateful, Ricky Wheeler."

"Hey, you're the one who gave me the idea in the first place. Remember that time you snuck me into the studio late at night to show me the brand new special effects that were being developed?"

"I *liked* you then," Jennifer returned bitterly. "You and I had just started going out, and I didn't know yet what kind of person you really are. I thought it would be fun to show you that cassette. I *trusted* you. It never occurred to me that you intended to steal it when you asked me if you could borrow it overnight so you could show it to your ten-year-old nephew. . . ."

"Yeah, you really bought that lie, didn't you?" Ricky grinned. "And now I've really got a good thing going."

Jennifer, the twins could see through the wooden slats, looked miserable. But it was obvious that she wasn't about to give Ricky the satisfaction of seeing her cry.

"Oh, yes. It's worked out fine—for *you*." Her tone was bitter. "But what would you do if I stopped sneaking those video cassettes out of Silver Screen Studios for you? Then what would happen to your profitable little 'business' of selling one studio's secrets to another?"

"You know exactly what would happen, sweetie pie. I've made that clear all along. I'd make it look as if your dear father was the one who'd been stealing studio secrets from Silver Screen Studios all along and selling them to Hollywood Productions—just as I've always promised I would."

"And you say you're not a blackmailer!" Jennifer spat out her words. "Here you are, threatening to ruin my father if I don't cooperate with you, telling me you'll destroy his twenty-five-year career, not to mention his good name, all because you want to make a lot of money fast, without doing a single thing to earn it."

"Such harsh words," Ricky said. "And here I

thought you and I were finally starting to become friends. But I'm afraid you're right. I would destroy your father's reputation, if I had to. I've got a good thing going here, and I'm not about to let you or anybody else screw it up.

"Besides," he went on with a shrug, "as long as nobody knows, as long as we continue to keep this arrangement of ours a secret, then everybody's happy."

"Oh, really?"

"Sure. I'm happy because I get all that wonderful money that Hollywood Productions is paying me for the information I'm giving them. My friends over at Hollywood Productions are happy because they're about to start making a film of their own, using almost identical special effects. Yes, their film should be able to compete with Silver Screen's blockbuster quite nicely, when they're both released within days of each other."

"Right." Jennifer snorted. "And I'm sure these 'friends' of yours will have absolutely no qualms about pretending that *they're* the ones who were clever enough to develop those innovative special effects."

Ricky just smiled. "I wouldn't be surprised. Anyway, I know that you're happy with our little deal because I'm doing what I promised I would do, which is keep your father's name completely out of this. So, as I said, nobody gets hurt—well, almost nobody. And some of us are profiting quite nicely."

"You swine!" Jennifer cried. She picked up a book from a table nearby and hurled it at him. "I'm tempted to stop going along with you in this dishonest little escapade of yours and just see what you do."

"Call my bluff, huh? Well, take my advice, sister. Don't even *think* about it. Because if you start playing games with me, I'll see to it that your daddy ends up behind bars."

With that, Ricky turned away and stalked out of the room, slamming the door behind him. As soon as she was certain that he was really gone, Jennifer sank onto the couch and burst into tears.

Impulsively Chris pushed open the wooden doors, not even hearing the loud gasp that Susan let out when she realized what her sister was about to do.

"Jennifer . . ." said Chris, her voice soft so as not to startle her.

Jennifer's expression turned to one of shock as her tears were forgotten. "You two—again. What are you doing here?" This time, she seemed to be more confused than angry.

"Jennifer, listen to us, please," Chris begged. "Don't be upset. Yes, I'm afraid we were eavesdropping. But you *do* want us to help you, don't you? Isn't that why you sent us that magazine article?"

"I never . . . oh, dear. Of course you're right. I am the one who sent you that article."

"We understand now why you did," Susan said. "It all makes sense. Ricky's been blackmailing you, having you steal cassettes from Silver Screen

Studios so he can sell them to Hollywood Productions, telling you he'll destroy your father if you don't cooperate. What I don't understand is, why have you been so unwilling to let us help you expose him for what he is?"

"Because I'm *afraid*," Jennifer blurted out. "Chris, Susan, if he knew I'd sent you that magazine clipping, if he knew I was even *talking* to someone who knew about this matter—why, I'm afraid that he'd go ahead with the threats he's been making all along. He would make it look as if my father had been selling Silver Screens Studios' secrets to one of its competitors. And even if he could prove that he was innocent, the scandal would destroy him—and his career."

"But Jennifer!" Chris pleaded. "Couldn't you just . . ."

"Ricky Wheeler is a very dangerous person," Jennifer insisted. "In fact, I want you two to leave right now. He might come back, or . . . or he might even have this place bugged, for all I know. I never should have taken the risk of sending you that magazine article! If he ever found out . . . please, go away. None of this is your problem—and if you know what's good for you, you'll keep it that way. Just leave me alone."

Chris and Susan exchanged rueful glances, and then, slowly and reluctantly, headed toward the front door. Their hearts felt as if they were made of lead as they dragged themselves back toward the car.

And neither of them could figure out what was worse: the reality of what was happening to poor Jennifer Franklin, or the fact that without her cooperation, the twins couldn't do a single thing about it.

Eight

"Now *what?*" With a loud groan, Chris dropped onto her large colorful beach towel, digging her toes into the fine white sand.

The twins' discussion with Jennifer the night before had left both Chris and Susan totally discouraged about the Popcorn Project. They'd stayed up late, talking it over, finally coming to the conclusion that no matter how they tried, Jennifer's refusal to cooperate with them in any way was going to make it impossible for them to help her.

And so the girls had decided to forget all about Mr. Franklin and Jennifer. Early in the morning, they put on their bathing suits, packed themselves a picnic lunch, and drove off in their aunt's car to Venice, a scenic seaside town on the outer edge of Los Angeles that was known as much for the colorful characters that could be found there as for its exquisite beach.

So far, it had been a perfectly lovely day. After strolling through the picturesque town, browsing in some of the shops that lined the ocean front and enjoying the muscle-builders working out on the sand and the roller skaters twirling by on the sidewalks, Susan and Chris had headed down to the water. Susan lathered up with sun-tan lotion and lay down in the sun with an enjoyable paperback novel. Meanwhile, Chris raced toward the ocean right away, anxious to have another swim in the Pacific.

Yet when she emerged from the waves, instead of looking relaxed and carefree, she interrupted her sister's quiet mood with her woeful question.

"Now what?" Susan repeated, glancing up from her book. "Well, we could go for a walk along the surf. Or we could break open our picnic lunch. Or we could just lie here, without moving a single muscle. . . ."

"That's not what I meant," Chris interrupted, grabbing a towel. She began to dry her hair, her movements so energetic that she sprayed her twin with a light mist of salt water.

"Hey, watch out! You're getting me wet—and that water is *cold*."

"Good." Chris peered out from underneath her towel, grinning. "Maybe a little cold water will help you snap out of your discouraged mood."

With a loud sigh, Susan closed her book and rolled over on her side so that she was facing her twin sister. "Christine Pratt, I'm afraid I haven't got the slightest idea what you're talking about."

"Why, I'm talking about the Popcorn Project, of course!"

"The Popcorn Project! Wait a minute. Did I imagine this, or did you and I decide—what, not twelve hours ago—that the Popcorn Project was *hopeless*? That even though we finally found out what was going on with Jennifer, the fact that she's refused to help us, or even let us tell her father what's going on, has made it impossible for the Popcorn Project to proceed any further?"

Susan shook her head sadly. "She's afraid, Chris—and to tell you the truth, I don't blame her. I'd be scared, too, if I were in her shoes."

"Yes, I probably would be, too," Chris agreed. "But even though the odds are against us, that doesn't mean you're *really* ready to give up . . . does it?"

"I thought it did," Susan said meekly, "up until about three minutes ago. . . ."

"Good. That means you're ready to have your mind changed, then."

Susan peered at her twin. "Are you saying that you've come up with an idea, Chris?"

Chris thought for a minute, still drying her hair. By now, however, her movements were slow and thoughtful.

"Nope," she finally admitted. "I don't have a single idea of where to proceed from here. But that doesn't mean I've given up hoping."

"I must confess, I've been thinking about little else besides Jennifer Franklin and her plight ever since last night. I even *dreamed* about her—and that awful Ricky Wheeler and what he's doing to her. Imagine, blackmail! Why, that's serious business."

"I know," Chris said grimly. "And I'd give anything to help Jennifer—and help put that weasel in jail."

"Oh, if only Jennifer would help us." Susan sighed. "Without her to help us get proof, the Popcorn Project is at a dead end."

"I know." Chris thought for a minute. "Boy, if only we could have taped that little scene between her and Ricky that we witnessed last night. That would have been proof enough for anyone— including a court of law."

"Right. Next time I'm eavesdropping on somebody else's conversation, Chris, I'll be sure I've brought along my tape recorder."

"Or do you know what would be even better? If we could have *filmed* that discussion they had. Then there would have been no doubt as to Ricky Wheeler's guilt."

"Well, it's too late now. That is, unless we could get Jennifer and Ricky to reenact that scene, all over again."

"Hah!" Chris snorted. "Maybe we could if she'd cooperate with us. I mean, if she would only agree to meet with Ricky while you and I were—oh, I don't know, filming them both, without him knowing it, of course. . . ."

"That would be ideal!" For a moment, Susan brightened. But then she remembered the one fatal flaw in the plan that Chris was devising off the top of her head. "Only there's one major thing missing: Jennifer!"

She glanced over at her twin, expecting her to

look as upset about this as she was. Instead, Susan saw that Chris actually had a peculiar gleam in her eye—a look that could only mean one thing.

"Uh, oh. What is it, Chris? Don't tell me you've gotten another one of your brainstorms. . . ."

"Sooz, what did you just say?" Chris's voice sounded odd.

"Well, let's see. I guess what I said was that your plan of filming Jennifer and Ricky talking about the fact that he's blackmailing her would be an excellent way to expose him, except for the fact that Jennifer won't cooperate. That's right; I said that she's the only ingredient that's missing."

"That's right. She *is* the only ingredient that's missing."

Susan scowled. "But having her there would be the most important part of the plan. In fact, without her, there *is* no plan."

"That's true, too," Chris said. Considering the expression on her face, her voice sounded amazingly calm. "But what if she *were* there, letting us film her as she argued with Ricky . . . or if she weren't there, if somebody else that looked just like her was there? Someone who looked so much like her, in fact, that even Ricky couldn't tell the difference?"

"That would be the solution to all our problems, Chris. Unfortunately, there's only *one* Jennifer Franklin. She doesn't have an identical twin, the way you and I do."

"Oh, no? Doesn't she?" Chris was smiling mischievously. "Doesn't *everyone* have an identical twin—or at least the *possibility* of having one? That is, if they're willing to try the kind of special effects that are Henry Hartley's specialty."

"Christine Pratt, would you *please* tell me what on earth you're *talking* about?" By this point, Susan was growing much too impatient with her sister's mysteriousness. Obviously, Chris thought she had come up with a solution . . . and Susan was not about to wait forever to hear about it.

"Sooz," Chris said, leaning forward and talking in a whisper so that no one else would be able to hear, "if you and I need Jennifer Franklin to help us, we'll just have to sneak into Silver Screen Studios' special effects department and make our *own* Jennifer Franklin."

Susan's mouth dropped open. "Wait a minute. You're suggesting that we make a *mask* that looks like Jennifer, and then have one of us pose as her in order to trap Ricky into confessing on camera?"

Chris's smile was triumphant. "You've hit the nail on the head. One of us can pretend to be Jennifer while the other one films the conversation she'll be having with Ricky! When we go to the police, it won't matter that our 'Jennifer' is a fake. What *will* matter is that we have good solid evidence that Ricky Wheeler is a blackmailer. After all, what better proof than a film on him confessing to the crime?"

"Christine Pratt, this is brilliant." Suddenly Susan's expression changed to a pensive frown. "Do you really think we could do it, though? First, wc'd have to get Jennifer to agree to let us make a mask of her face. We'd have to come up with some excuse. . . ."

"No sweat," her twin assured her with a confident wave of her hand. "You know as well as I do that when you and I put our minds together, that kind of thing is a snap."

"Okay. Assuming we get her to agree, we have to *make* the mask."

"That's your department. But I have every confidence in you, Sooz! Between your artistic ability and the fact that you watched Henry make a mask only days ago . . . Well, all we have to do is convince good old Max to let us into the special effects studio when no one else is around. Maybe we could even get him to help us out. After all, he *is* an expert."

"Okay. So there we are with a mask of Jennifer Franklin . . . and we arrange a meeting between our fake 'Jennifer' and Ricky, preferably at the studio, where we can film their entire conversation."

"See that? It'll be as easy as pie."

"Well, I wouldn't go *that* far. . . ."

Chris could see that her sister still had some doubts. "Sooz, I know as well as you do that there's a lot of uncertainty in this plan. A lot of risk, too. But if we want to help Jennifer—and I'm certain that you feel as strongly about that as I do—it's our only chance."

In the face of this logic, it didn't take long for Susan to make up her mind. After all, Chris was right on both counts. It was true that she was as committed to helping Jennifer as her twin was. And it was equally true that, without Jennifer's help, they *were* in a bind—and Chris's plan, however uncertain, however risky, was their only hope.

"There you go again, Chris," Susan finally said, a teasing tone covering up her nervousness. "Being *right*. Of course we'll go ahead with your plan."

Chris just looked at her and smiled.

Chris and Susan both realized at this point that a little bit of acting was going to be required in order to continue with the Popcorn Project. What they needed to do now was get this reluctant young woman to agree to let them make a mask that would duplicate her face—step one of the final phase of the Popcorn Project, and the only contribution that Jennifer would be required to make in order for them to proceed with their scheme.

"I still feel a little bit sneaky," Susan whispered as she and her twin knocked on the door of the Franklins' house. "I mean, we *are* going to be telling Jennifer something that isn't quite true. . . ."

"Think of it this way," Chris countered, sounding matter-of-fact. "We're just *stretching* the truth a little bit. And if you like, you can leave the whole thing to me. I'm so convinced that we're doing the right thing that I'll have no problem with our little deception. Just wait until you see me in action!"

When Jennifer answered the door and her expression changed from a pleasant one to one of alarm, Susan was only too happy to leave step one to her sister who, she was convinced, was not only braver, but was also a much better actress.

"Hello, Jennifer." Chris sounded completely calm. "Yes, I know you're surprised to see us. But this time we're here on a friendly mission."

"What do you mean, 'a friendly mission?'" Jennifer eyed her two uninvited guests suspiciously.

"It has something to do with the big celebration to honor your father tomorrow night. Is it okay if Sooz and I come in for a few minutes to tell you about this brainstorm we came up with?"

Jennifer hesitated.

"It's a great idea," Susan piped up, unable to resist. "Something that your father will love. In fact, it's practically guaranteed to be the highlight of his entire evening."

Still somewhat reluctant, Jennifer moved aside so that the twins could come in. Chris walked inside the house and plopped onto the couch, making herself right at home. Susan followed, sitting down gingerly on a chair.

"Here's the plan, Jennifer," Chris said heartily. "Among all the people who will be standing up and making speeches about your father's tremendous contribution to the motion picture industry over the past twenty-five years will be his daughter.

"I can see it all now." Her brown eyes took on a dreamy, faraway look. "Jennifer Franklin talks about all the various aspects of movies that he's helped—last but not least being the area of special effects. And then, at the end, just when everyone is starting to applaud, she pulls off her mask—and she's not Jennifer at all, but one of us—wearing a mask that's identical to Jennifer's face!"

She paused, looking over at Susan for approval. "Well, what do you think? Isn't it fabulous?"

Jennifer thought for a few seconds. "Gee, I don't know. I guess it's . . . different."

"Different? It's *unique*! And the best thing about it," Chris went on, bursting with confidence, "is that this whole thing embodies the whole point of movies! They capture people's imaginations, take them out of themselves, lead them into the wonderful world of make-believe, where anything can—and *does*—happen. . . ."

"I'm just as excited about this as Chris is," Susan interjected. "Please say yes, Jennifer. I just know your father would get a real kick out of it!"

"Well, who would make the mask? And when?"

The twins could tell that they were winning her over.

"Oh, Sooz here has gobs of experience making masks," Chris insisted.

"I wouldn't say *gobs*, exactly."

But Chris wasn't about to let Susan's protests influence Jennifer. "Aw, Sooz, you're just being modest. Why, you're practically a professional! As for the when, we can do it this evening."

"This evening! Hmmm. Yes, I suppose we would have to get started right away, since my father's celebration is in only twenty-four hours. . . ."

Suddenly all her doubts seemed to vanish. Jennifer flashed her pretty smile, then said, "Okay, you're on! I think it's a wonderful idea. And I'm willing to do just about anything to make my father's special celebration a success."

"Great," said Chris. "I'll tell you what: meet us at the Silver Screen Studios special effects building in an hour. And wear old clothes. That plaster can get a little messy."

"Gee, you were right," Susan said admiringly as the girls drove off, ready to begin step two. "It *was* a cinch! Jennifer believed every word you said."

Chris grimaced. "I only hope I can be as convincing where Max is concerned."

"I'm not a bit worried," Susan returned with a chuckle. "Maybe it's being out here in Hollywood, but I've never seen your acting abilities stronger!"

Those abilities were put to the test once again as the two girls approached Max's office. After all, they needed his permission to use the special-effects studio. And they still hoped they could talk him into helping them make the mask. And so Chris was at her most charming as she and Susan sailed into his office.

"Hello, again! Remember us?"

The chubby, bald-headed man looked up from the robot he was tinkering with and squinted at these two intruders through his thick eyeglasses. "Can't say I do. Do I know you girls?"

"You certainly do! We were here just yesterday. Henry Hartley brought us over to show us how those wonderful masks are made."

"Oh, yes. Now I remember." He turned back to his robot. "Is there something I can help you with?"

Chris acted surprised. "You mean Henry didn't tell you?"

"Tell me what?"

"That he wanted us to come in tonight and help him out by making another one of those masks."

"Nope. Henry didn't say a word. Hey, what's it for, anyway?"

Chris's face suddenly looked blank. "I . . . uh . . . it's . . ."

Susan couldn't help coming to her twin's rescue. "Come on, Chris. We might as well tell Max the truth."

"The truth?" Chris swallowed hard.

"That's right, the truth." Susan turned to Max and said, "You know that celebration that Silver Screen Studios is having for Donald Franklin tomorrow night?"

"Sure do. I'm one of the lucky ones who's been invited, and I can hardly wait."

"Well, then. I'm sorry to have to spoil the big surprise of the evening, but . . ."

"Wait! Don't tell me!" Max threw up his hands. "If it's a surprise, and it has to do with Don Franklin, a man's who's never treated me with anything but kindness and respect . . . well, that's all I have to know. Girls, the studio is yours. And please let me know it there's anything I can do to help."

"Well, Max," said Chris, "now that you mention it. . . ."

Late that night, after having spent several hours finishing up Jennifer's mask with Max's assistance, the twins successfully completed step three of their plan. Chris telephoned Ricky at home, pretending that her strange, hoarse voice really belonged to

Jennifer Franklin—with a bad cold. When she told him she had something important to discuss with him, and that she wanted to meet him at the studio at ten the next morning, he agreed without giving it a second thought.

"Wow! All this has been even easier than I thought." Chris said triumphantly as she and Susan climbed into bed, exhausted but at the same time exhilarated.

"I'll say," her sister agreed. "So far, you're batting a thousand on even the most difficult parts."

"Difficult? Are you kidding? This has been the *easy* part." As the two girls talked in the dark, Chris's voice sounded strained. "Hold on to your hat, Sooz. Come tomorrow, you and I tackle the hard stuff. The Popcorn Project is about to shift into step four—maybe the riskiest, scariest, most difficult thing you and I have ever tried."

Nine

Saturday morning wasn't the first morning in her life that Chris had woken up with butterflies in her stomach. On many occasions she had lain awake in bed, nervous as she thought about the day ahead.

Today, however, she was particularly apprehensive. This was, after all, the morning of the final steps of the Popcorn Project. There was still a lot of uncertainty involved—not to mention a lot of risk.

First, she had to convince Ricky Wheeler that she was Jennifer Franklin. That, in itself, was going to be quite a challenge. Second, Susan was going to have to figure out how to work the cameras at Silver Screen Studios—again, no easy task.

The third issue was so overwhelming that she barely dared think about it: when you came right down to it, the twins didn't really know just how dangerous a person Ricky Wheeler was—and what he would do if, somehow, he found out he was being tricked.

But her past experiences had taught Chris that there was nothing to be gained by stewing over things she couldn't control. Instead, she had learned, it was better to concentrate on simply doing her very best. She reminded herself of this, then hopped out of bed, ready to wake up her sister.

Susan, however, had already been up for quite a while, thanks to her own flock of bothersome butterflies. As Chris emerged from the bedroom, she was surprised to find her dressed and in the kitchen, whipping up a batch of pancakes. Aunt Karen, sitting at the table with a cup of tea, looked up and gave Chris a pleasant smile.

"Good morning, sleepyhead. You certainly slept late for someone who's about to embark on a very exciting day!"

Chris cast her twin a questioning look. After all, the girls had agreed yesterday that in order to make this final stage of the Popcorn Project work, no one, including their aunt, would be told about it.

But Susan was quick to explain. "I told Aunt Karen that we're cooking up a special surprise for Mr. Franklin's celebration tonight. Of course," she added, "I didn't tell her exactly what it was. . . ."

"That's right," Karen said cheerfully. "All I could get out of your twin here was that you and Jennifer put your heads together and came up with something that's bound to be the hit of the evening. Oh, and she also told me that you two have to sneak into Silver Screen Studios today to take care of some last-minute details."

Chris just nodded, afraid of saying the wrong thing. Then she sat down at the table and attacked a huge stack of pancakes, having decided that while she wasn't really hungry, today was a day that she would need every ounce of her energy and strength.

"Gee, you really scared me," Chris whispered after breakfast, as she dried the breakfast dishes that her sister was washing. "For a minute there, I thought you'd told Aunt Karen about our plan."

"Not quite," Susan replied. "But I figured somebody should know where we were going today, in case something went wrong."

"Wrong?" Chris said jokingly, trying to hide the effect that her sister's words had had on her. "My goodness, Sooz. You and I are practically *professionals*, remember? What could possibly go wrong?"

A few hours later, that question was still lurking at the back of their minds as Chris and Susan drove into the parking lot of Silver Screen Studios. Chris was clutching a small shopping bag that contained everything she would need: her Jennifer Franklin disguise, a handkerchief, and a hand-written letter that she had composed that morning.

Since it was Saturday, there was no actual filming going on, but the usual tours were in full swing. The twins had no difficulty blending in with the crowds of tourists, and since they knew their way around, they made it to their first stop without any problems.

Fortunately, the employees' lounge was empty. Quickly each one of the girls grabbed one of the kelly-green uniforms piled up near the door, the ones the tour guides wore, and slipped into them. That way, they had decided earlier, they would be less likely to be stopped as they sneaked into their final destination, Studio B, where they had told Ricky to meet Jennifer promptly at ten o'clock.

The twins' luck held out. They managed to get into the deserted building without hitting any snags. Now it was time to confront some of the technical difficulties of their plan. Chris snapped on the lights and found that everything looked exactly as it had the other time the girls had been in here. Only this time, they saw it all differently. They couldn't help being overwhelmed, more than a little bit dismayed, as they studied the cavernous room filled with wires, cables, tremendous lights, and a complex array of cameras and other equipment, all set up around the stage. Susan let out a loud groan.

"Chris, how on *earth* am I ever going to figure out how to work these cameras? Look at them! Why, some of them are as big as I am! Quite a far cry from my little instamatic. How am I ever going to film you and Ricky with one of these monsters?"

"Gee, Sooz. I'm afraid I can't help you there." Chris's regret was sincere as she looked up from her own preparations. She was busy putting on the green-tinted contact lenses and blond wig she had borrowed from the special-effects studio, along with the nearly perfect Jennifer Franklin mask that Max and her sister had made with impressive skill.

"But you'd better hurry up and figure something out. According to my watch, Ricky is due here in about another eight minutes."

Frantically Susan went from one huge camera to another, trying to find one that looked manageable. She was all ready to give up, to tell Chris that this final and most important step of the Popcorn Project wasn't going to work after all, when something caught her eye. Sitting on a shelf was a small video camera, the kind that some of her friends' parents had started buying recently in order to film home movies—movies with sound.

"Chris, I think our worries are over," Susan breathed, almost afraid to pick it up and see if it had any film inside. When she finally did, she let out a cry of relief. "Yes, this is perfect. Chris, we're all set!"

"Good thing," Chris returned, her voice a hoarse whisper, "because I think somebody's coming."

Sure enough; the silhouette of a sloppily dressed young man appeared in the doorway just as Susan ducked behind some large equipment, her video camera in hand. Chris, meanwhile, sat down on a chair in the middle of the stage, clutching the handkerchief she had brought in one hand and the folded piece of paper in the other.

From where she was crouching, Susan could see that her sister did, indeed, look like Jennifer Franklin. Even in the bright lights they had turned on, the kind used for filming real movies, the face was identical to Jennifer's. With the contact lenses and the long blond wig, as well as the kelly-green uniform that Ricky was already used to seeing her in, she would have no trouble passing herself off as the other girl.

The only possible problem was the voice. But Chris had thought of everything. As Ricky came over, walking with his usual swagger, she held the handkerchief up to her face and pretended to be crying.

"H-hello, Ricky," she said, her voice muffled by both the handkerchief and her fake sobs.

Chris, you're doing a great job! Susan thought proudly. Lights, cameras, action . . . we're ready to roll!

With that, she switched on the video camera and began to film Ricky and "Jennifer's" conversation.

"Yeah, so what was so important that you had to see me today, Jennifer?" Ricky demanded in a gruff voice.

"H-here. Read this." Without looking at him, Chris-as-Jennifer handed him the note.

"What's this?" Frowning, he began to read.

"Read it out loud."

Ricky glanced over at the girl beside him, then began to read. "To the Editor of the *Los Angeles Star*. I am writing to expose a terrible blackmail plot, in which Ricky Wheeler has been forcing me, Jennifer Franklin, to steal video cassettes of newly developed special effects created at Silver Screen Studios so that he could sell them to one of the studio's competitors, Hollywood Productions. . . ." Hey, wait a minute. What is this?"

"Everything it says in that letter is true, isn't it?"

"Well, sure it's true, although you know I don't like the word 'blackmail.' "

Susan leaned forward, gleeful as she filmed both Ricky's face and every word he was saying.

"So what is this, anyway? You mean you're actually planning to *send* this letter?"

"M-m-maybe," Chris-as-Jennifer sobbed.

"Hey, wait a minute. What are you, crazy? You mean you're going to end this sweet little deal you and I have got going? Hollywood Productions has been paying me good money for those stolen tapes. You think I'm just going to stand by and let you ruin this? Maybe even get myself put in jail?"

"And what if I do?"

"You know darn well what I'll do. Exactly what I've been telling you all along. I'll say that it's your father who's been stealing those tapes, not me. After all, he's a top executive here at Silver Screen Studios, with access to all their secrets. Who would ever expect a nobody like me to be mixed up in something like this? But your father . . . yeah, it'd be a piece of cake to put it all on him. He'd be ruined."

Once again, Susan crept a little bit closer, wanting to make sure she got it all on film.

"Besides," Ricky went on smugly, "you've got absolutely no proof that I've been involved in this."

All of a sudden, there was a loud crash. Susan had leaned forward just a little bit too much, knocking over the huge camera she had been hiding behind. Before she had a chance to grab it, it fell to the floor.

"What the heck . . . ?" Ricky looked over just in time to see Susan standing a few feet away from him, filming every word he was saying. "Wait a minute! You mean you've been *filming* this? Why, you . . . !"

Ricky lunged for the girl he thought was Jennifer, having understood in a fraction of a second exactly what was going on. Susan, meanwhile, realized just as quickly that their filming session was over. She took the film out of the camera, slipped it into the front pocket of her kelly-green uniform, and made a mad dash toward the door.

"Run, run!" she cried. "He's after us!"

Her warning was unnecessary. Chris, still looking like Jennifer Franklin, was two steps behind her, with Ricky on her tail. Fortunately, the two girls were agile, much better than he was at stepping over the thick wires and cables that covered this section of the studio floor.

"Quick. This way," Susan commanded. She headed through the first doorway she reached. The twins raced inside, closing the heavy door behind them.

"Lock it," cried Chris.

Susan was only too happy to comply.

"Now what do we do?" Chris whispered. There was panic in her voice.

"We'll think of something," Susan reassured her, not believing her own words. "At any rate, I've got the film right here." She patted her pocket.

"Great. Now all we have to do is come up with a way to get ourselves and the film out of this mess." Desperately, Chris glanced around her. "Hey, where are we, anyway?"

In the dim light she could see that this was not a closet, as she had at first assumed, but a large room that seemed to extend on forever. In it there were large tables, as if this were a work room of some kind. Along the edges there were big bulky things, all shapes and sizes, looking ominous in the shadows.

Suddenly Chris brightened. "Hey! Do you know where we are, Sooz?"

"I don't care," Susan returned. "All I want to know is how we're going to get *out* of here."

"Sooz, look! We're in the special-effects laboratory! This is where we made the mask!"

"So what? I'm hardly in the mood for being creative right now!"

"But don't you see? 'Being creative' is *exactly* how we can get out of here."

Susan thought for a few seconds, then smiled. "I think I'm starting to understand. But what exactly is your idea?"

Chris frowned. "I don't know yet. But let's take a look around."

Being careful to be quiet, as well as to hurry, the twins took a quick survey of the special-effects lab. Chris darted among the props, looking for inspiration, while Susan began an organized study, slowly checking out each item she came across.

And then, suddenly, there was a huge crash.

"Look out!" Chris cried, scrambling to hide behind a cabinet. "Ricky's breaking down the door!"

She was right. It was only a matter of seconds before he came rushing in, his hands curled into angry fists, his face twisted into a snarl. And there was Susan, standing right in the middle of the room, in plain sight.

"There you are, you little . . ."

As Ricky came running toward her, Susan looked around for something—anything—to throw at him. She grabbed the first thing she saw, an odd-looking object sitting on a table. She hurled it at him, hoping to distract him for at least a few seconds. And then, before she knew what had happened, there was a tremendous explosion, right before her eyes.

What on earth . . . ! she thought, not able to comprehend what had happened. Even so, she had the presence of mind to start running in the opposite direction. When she finally looked over her shoulder, she saw that Ricky had fallen to the ground. For a moment she feared that she had really hurt him, and her first instinct was to rush over to help him. But the words he uttered prompted her to keep running.

"What the—what's this, a phony grenade?" Angrier than ever, he started up the chase once again.

Susan kept running, now looking for something to throw in his path. She noticed a hulking metallic robot standing alongside the wall. Quickly she pulled it smack into the middle of the aisle, meanwhile accidentally pushing the "start" button.

As she raced ahead, she could hear it uttering in

its mechanical voice, "Welcome to our planet! Welcome to our planet!" Glancing over her shoulder, she saw it waving its huge arms as bright lights flashed on and off—just the thing to slow Ricky down as he was forced to wrestle with this automatic monster that blocked his path.

But now, Susan was almost at the end of the long room. She had no idea where Chris was—probably hiding, she guessed, and in a lot less danger than she was. But there was no time to worry about that now, not when she was about to be cornered at the end of the lab.

Then she spotted a door, rusted over so badly that it looked as if it might never open again. Nevertheless, she rushed over to it. Her heart pounding wildly, she yanked on the handle as hard as she could.

Please open, she thought. Please . . . please. . . .

To her great relief, she felt the door move as she pulled. She stepped through the doorway—and found herself on a small ledge. She stopped herself just in time, gasping as she looked down and saw that below her was a big drop, at least twenty-five feet. She blinked and struggled to get her bearings, finally realizing that she was back in Studio B—or, she noted grimly, at the very top of Studio B. Stretching beyond the ledge on which she was standing was the rickety-looking bridge, the one made of rough-hewn rope and wooden slats. It reached over to the other side, about thirty feet across, where there was another ledge.

Susan's impulse was to dash across the bridge,

but something inside her warned that it simply wasn't safe. It was old, and in very poor condition. Besides, for all she knew, it had never been strong enough to hold anyone in the first place. Maybe it was just a prop. . . .

She had only a split second to make her decision. She could hear Ricky's footsteps, coming up behind her. She had two choices: to stay where she was and risk being caught, or to try the bridge.

She glanced at the narrow wooden slats, held together with frayed rope. It was simply too dangerous, she decided. She crouched down on the ledge, back along the wall on one side of the doorway. That way, she would at least be out of sight.

Susan closed her eyes, knowing that it was only a question of seconds before Ricky found her. After all, he, too, would undoubtedly conclude that the bridge wasn't strong enough to hold him.

And then Ricky was standing in the doorway, having paused to catch his breath. While Susan could see him from where she was kneeling, he hadn't yet looked down and noticed her. Instead, she could see, he was staring at the rickety wooden bridge before him, no doubt evaluating whether or not it was safe.

And then, all of a sudden, something on the other end of Studio B caught Susan's eye. She looked over and saw that standing there, at the far end of the bridge, was a girl who looked just like her, with the same face and hair and the same kelly-green uniform, standing tauntingly with her hand on one hip.

"What's the matter, Ricky?" Chris yelled across the cavernous studio. "Scared? If this bridge was strong enough to hold me, don't you think you dare take a chance? " She patted her front pocket. "Look, I've got the film I shot right here. Why don't you come on over and get it?"

"Why, you . . ." With that, Ricky went darting across the bridge, chasing after the girl he thought was the same one he had been chasing all along. But he had only gone about halfway across when there was a loud *snap*. One of the frayed ropes had given way. Within a fraction of a second the wooden slats began to tumble off—and Ricky began to lose his balance.

"Whoa!" he cried, his voice echoing through the huge studio. "I'm going to fall . . . !"

Chris and Susan, standing on two different ledges at opposite edges of the studio, watched in horror as Ricky went tumbling down, yelling at the top of his lungs. Their bodies were tense as they waited to hear the loud crash that said he had hit the ground.

Instead, all they heard was a soft *thump*—and then a low moan.

"Ricky! Are you all right?" called Chris, suddenly afraid of what her little stunt might have caused. She peered down from the edge, but she couldn't see anything.

"Where *am* I?" he cried in a muffled voice. He sounded more puzzled than anything else.

"Are you hurt?" Susan yelled. She, too, was trying desperately to figure out what had happened.

"I'm in some kind of *cage* or something," came Ricky's reply. "Except it's made out of bamboo. . . . Hey, I'm stuck! Get me out of here, will you?"

Across Studio B, Chris and Susan looked at each other—and burst out laughing.

"It looks like we caught our prey!" Chris finally said.

"And it's a lot better than a lion!" Susan replied, still chuckling.

"Hey, get me out of here, will you?" Ricky pleaded. "I'm telling you, I'm locked into this thing."

"Good!" said Susan. "That's exactly where you belong for now. Sorry we can't help you, but we've got more important things to do." Looking across at her sister, she said merrily, "Chris, I assume there's a way for you to get down on your side . . . ?"

"There sure is," Chris replied. "After Ricky came barging into the special effects lab, chasing you, I went out the door he came in. I followed a long hallway and found myself on this ledge. Meanwhile, I'd taken off my mask and that wig. . . . To tell you the truth, it was just sheer luck that I ended up in the right place at the right time!"

"Are you kidding?" Susan cried. "Haven't you learned yet that we Pratt twins never solve our cases through luck? It's all the result of brain power—and some pretty good planning.

"Now, you and I have got a date with the Los Angeles Police Department," she went on, patting her pocket and discovering, much to her relief, that the film was still safe inside. "I have a feeling that the movie we're about to show them is going to be one they'll find fascinating. So fascinating, in fact, that they won't even need popcorn to enjoy it."

Ten

"*Well, you two certainly pulled off a real surprise* for my father tonight," said Jennifer Franklin, beaming at her two new friends. "Something a lot more impressive than that silly practical joke you pretended you were planning. Imagine, you actually got Ricky Wheeler's confession on video tape."

"And it was some confession, too," said Mr. Franklin. "To think he's been blackmailing my daughter, threatening to ruin me if she didn't cooperate with him in his crooked little scheme. . . . Well, I don't know what would have happened if you girls hadn't stepped in." He put a protective arm around his daughter, then leaned over and kissed the top of her head.

It was Saturday night, and the party celebrating Donald Franklin's twenty-five years at Silver

Screen Studios was just getting underway. Chris and Susan were standing next to the guest of honor as he greeted the people coming into the elegant restaurant in which the event was being held, a French bistro that was considered one of Los Angeles's very finest. Jennifer was on his other side, saying hello to many old friends and acquaintances, as well as meeting some new ones. Henry Hartley and Bruce Jackson were also at the party, at the moment getting sodas for the girls.

"I don't know how we can ever thank you," Jennifer said. "You were both so much braver than I was. I was just too afraid of what Ricky might do. Instead, I went along with him, not knowing how else to protect my father. . . ."

"We never blamed you for a minute," Susan was quick to assure her. "After all, nobody knows as well as we do what a ruthless character Ricky Wheeler really is."

"I'll say," Chris agreed. "In fact, one of the best parts of tonight's celebration is knowing that he's in jail right now."

"And don't forget that there's a big story on this breaking in tomorrow morning's *Los Angeles Star*," Aunt Karen reminded them all, coming up behind them on her crutches. "I've already made sure of that."

"If this were a movie," Jennifer said with a contented sigh, "it would definitely be one with a happy ending."

"Speaking of movies," Mr. Franklin interjected, looking over at Chris and Susan with a twinkle in his eyes, "there's something I've been wanting to talk to you two about."

"What's that?" asked Susan.

"Do either of you have any acting experience?"

Chris and Susan both started laughing.

"Are you kidding?" said Chris, still chuckling. "How do you think Sooz and I managed to carry off the Popcorn Project? Why, we Pratt twins are practically professionals."

"Good. That's what I thought. Because I've been wondering if you two might do me another favor."

"Daddy!" Jennifer cried. "Haven't Susan and Chris already done enough for us?"

"Well, maybe." Mr. Franklin frowned. "I guess it would be too much to ask that they agree to play small roles in the movie we're shooting over at Silver Screen Studios right now. . . ."

Susan and Chris's mouths both dropped open.

"A *movie*?" cried Chris.

"You want us to be in a movie?" Susan repeated, barely able to believe what she was hearing.

Mr. Franklin laughed. "So I guess it's not such a bad idea after all, huh?"

"We'd love it!" Suddenly Chris grew serious. "There's just one thing, though."

"Really? What's that?"

"It had better not be a science-fiction movie," Chris insisted in a teasing voice. "If I have to wear an orange nose and green horns . . ."

"Don't worry," Mr. Franklin reassured them. "You'll both get to wear long, beautiful dresses in this one. And I'll bet you'll be the second-best-looking young women in Hollywood."

"Second-best?" Aunt Karen repeated, pretending to be annoyed. "And who, may I ask, is prettier than my two lovely nieces?"

"Why, my daughter, of course." Donald Franklin hugged Jennifer once again. "After all, the auditions for the newest Silver Screen Studios production are over now. All the casting decisions have been made. And the starring role is going to a newcomer, none other than Ms. Jennifer Franklin."

"Oh, Daddy! You mean I'm finally going to be in a movie? Thank you!"

"Don't thank me. I honestly had nothing to do with it. You earned this part, completely on your own."

"Oh, boy," Chris said to Susan. "We're going to be in a movie! And so is Jennifer. Things can't get much better than this. . . ."

Their pleasant conversation was suddenly interrupted by a flash of lights and a great rush of people toward the door.

"What happened?" Susan asked, confused.

"Oh, nothing much," said Mr. Franklin, craning his neck to see what all the fuss was about. "I suppose some of the big names have started to arrive at my little party, that's all."

Chris and Susan stood on tiptoe so that they could get a better look. Out in the street, in front of the restaurant, half a dozen sleek black limousines had just pulled up. Climbing out of them were some of the most famous celebrities in Hollywood, actors and actresses that the twins had been seeing in movies and on television for years.

"Oh, my gosh," whispered Susan, scarcely able to believe what she was seeing. "Is this for real, or am I dreaming?"

But her twin was lost in dreams of her own.

"Movie stars!" she cried. "Look! Paul Newman. And there's Tom Cruise. And there's Molly Ringwald, my favorite actress! I've seen every one of her movies. Oh, my! They're coming over this way!"

"Of course," Mr. Franklin said gently. "They're all friends of mine."

"You mean we're actually going to get to *meet* them?" Chris looked as if she were about to faint.

"Why, yes. As a matter of fact, I've arranged for six of Hollywood's biggest stars to sit at your table this evening." Teasingly, he added, "That *is* okay, isn't it?"

"Unless my twin here faints from happiness first," Susan joked.

But Chris barely heard her comment. She was too busy fishing around in her purse, looking for a pen and a pad of paper.

About the Author

Cynthia Blair grew up on Long Island, earned her B.S. from Bryn Mawr College in Pennsylvania, and went on to get a M.S. in marketing from M.I.T. She worked as a marketing manager for food companies but now has abandoned the corporate life in order to write. She lives on Long Island with her husband, Richard Smith, and their son Jesse.